WHEN

ASHES

FALL

MARNI MANN

PRAISE FOR WHEN ASHES FALL

"A **breathtakingly beautiful** and deeply moving story. When Ashes Fall **owned my emotions** to the very last word." *—Jodi Ellen Malpas, #1 New York Times Best-Selling Author*

"Sucked in completely and jealous of such a **clever story**! You won't put this one down. Marni will have readers desperate for every **soul gripping** page..." *—Rachel Van Dyken, #1 New York Times Best-Selling Author*

"Every once in a while we come across that **rare book**. The one that reminds us of why we have the overpowering ache to read and feel. *When Ashes Fall* is one of those books! **Read it, live it, treasure it.**" *—TotallyBooked Blog*

"*When Ashes Fall* **gripped me** from page one. The layers of the story and the characters unfold **beautifully** and the payoff is more than I could have imagined. It will **break your heart** and put it back together again." *—Sarah, Frolic Media*

"I can honestly say this book is her **best work** to date!" *—Ratula, Bookgasms Book Blog*

Visit my website at: www.MarniSMann.com
Cover Designer: Letitia Hasser, R.B.A Designs
Editor: Jovana Shirley, Unforeseen Editing, www.unforeseenediting.com
Proofreader: Judy Zweifel, Judy's Proofreading, and Kaitie Reister
Introduction Quote: Melissa Mann

ISBN-13: 978-1790378418

For Irving and Honey.
Thank you for giving me Boston.
I hold it as close as the both of you.

PLAYLIST

"Like a River Runs"—*Bleachers, Sia*
"Only If for a Night"—*Florence + The Machine*
"Like That"—*Bea Miller*
"Better With You"—*Michl*
"Nevermind"—*Dennis Lloyd*
"Big God"—*Florence + The Machine*
"Arsonist's Lullabye"—*Hozier*
"Love into the Light"—*Kesha*

PART ONE

I always heard music. Beats, lyrics. I only had to listen to a song once before it started playing in my head.
One day ... the music stopped.

ONE

ALIX

PRESENT DAY

"NINE-ONE-ONE, WHAT'S YOUR EMERGENCY?" I said into the headset as I stared at the computer screen.

While I waited for a response, I sucked in a deep breath and rested my fingers on the keyboard, my thumb gently tapping the space bar but not hard enough to actually press it down. My body tensed. The tips of my toes ground into the bottom of my shoes.

It was a ritual.

One I repeated every time I answered a call.

"I'm at the Public Garden," the woman said. "And a man just fell off one of the benches. He's on the ground, screaming. You can probably hear him in the background. It looks like he hurt his arm or something."

Once I processed her description, my chest loosened.

The air I'd been holding in slowly made its way through my lips.

The tapping stopped.

"What's your name?" I asked.

"Why do you need that?"

"It's for our records and also so I know what to call you."

"I'm not comfortable with giving you my last name, but my first name is Rachel."

"Rachel," I repeated as I typed it into the system, "do you know the man's name?"

"I don't know him. I was just walking by with my boyfriend, and I saw it happen."

"Are you able to get close to him and ask if he's okay?"

"Look, I'm just calling out of courtesy. I don't have time to go over and assess the man."

Before I could respond, Rachel disconnected the call.

So, I finished typing up my notes and dispatched the emergency response team to the Public Garden. Before they even left the firehouse, they'd know the man could be suffering from a broken arm, shoulder, or even head trauma and that no other symptoms had been reported.

Once I finished all the coding, I logged off and removed the headset. Then, I took out my bag from the bottom drawer and reached inside for my cell. I found Rose's last text and started typing.

Me: I'm not going to make it. I'm exhausted.
Rose: If you don't show up, I'm going to walk to your townhouse and drag your ass out. It's your choice.
Me: I'm leaving work right now. See you in 15.
Rose: I got us a table outside, right in front. You can't miss me.

I put the phone back in my bag and stood from the desk, making my way through the call center. This was where most of the emergency and non-emergency calls were answered for each district of Boston. Where we worked eight-hour shifts and handled over a thousand calls a day.

I wondered if I'd have the same ritual tomorrow.

Or if I'd have a different one.

Or maybe I wouldn't have one at all.

That thought was interrupted when I heard, "Alix," as I walked by Marla's office.

I stopped reluctantly and turned around, backtracking until I was in her doorway. "Hey," I said, watching her smile as she got up from her chair.

Marla was an officer and had been supervising this department for the six years I'd been employed by the city. I'd met her while I was in the EMT recruit academy when I was first hired.

She wrapped her arms around my shoulders and hugged me. "I hope today went all right."

I closed my eyes and made sure she didn't hear me sigh.

This was what I hadn't wanted.

Along with the extra-big smiles from my coworkers when I had walked into the call center earlier today.

And the card that had been slipped into my desk, which I'd opened before my shift.

And the invitation to lunch I had declined.

It was all really unnecessary.

And way too much.

I squeezed her back because it was the right thing to do and said, "Yes, today went fine." Then, I immediately pulled away.

"I'll see you tomorrow?"

"Of course."

I wondered if tomorrow would feel different.

I thought about that as I made my way through the police headquarters.

This building was so busy with employees, many of whom I'd met. Maybe even close to all of them. If they saw me, they'd want me to stop walking. They'd want to talk.

Some might even want to hug me.

To avoid any type of contact, I took out my phone and held it to my ear, pretending to be in a serious conversation. At the same time, I stayed to the left side of each room I passed through and kept my face down.

That was everything I could do to go unnoticed.

I was flooded with relief when I made it out the front of the building without having to say a word and continued my trek to Ruggles station, hurrying into the train before the door shut.

Two stops.

That was how far it was to Back Bay station.

During the ride, I looped my arm around the metal pole and scrolled through one of my apps. I was only able to read a handful of status updates before Back Bay station was announced from the speakers.

Once I made my way outside, I went down Dartmouth Street until I reached the restaurant. Rose was right in front, just like she had said in her text. She was at a small, round table that had two glasses of red wine and a charcuterie board on top of it.

"*Hiii*," she said as I got closer and embraced me the second I reached her.

I didn't mind.

That was part of the reason I was here.

I even hugged her back as hard as I could.

Rose and I had been assigned as roommates our freshman year at Northeastern. I was a shy girl from southern Maine, who made the honor roll with ease and wanted to work in health care. I was also extremely inexperienced in partying. Rose was from South Boston. She came to college with a master's degree in drinking and could throw up the next morning without even smudging her lipstick.

We were complete opposites.

And, although we had both changed so much over the years, we were still closer than ever.

"Hi," I whispered back.

She was holding me so tightly; it was hard to breathe.

"Thanks for not canceling."

"Well, I tried," I admitted.

"You know, if you really didn't want to come tonight, I wouldn't have forced you."

"I know."

I moved to the other side of the table and sat across from her. Once I slung my bag over the corner of the chair, I lifted the wine glass, clicked it against hers, and took a sip.

Pinot noir.

She knew what I needed.

"To moments," she said as I swallowed.

Rose believed in celebrating them.

Always.

And, according to her, today was one.

"To moments," I repeated.

She took a drink from her glass, and then she crossed her arms over the table and leaned in closer. "Tell me all about your day. I want to hear every detail."

I had known this question was coming. That was partly why I'd wanted to cancel. "I woke up, went for a run, and went to work, and now, I'm meeting you. There's not much else to tell."

"Alix ..."

She didn't say my name in a reprimanding way.

She said it as though she were encouraging me to talk about it. Because Rose forever assumed I needed to get something off my chest.

"Work was fine," I said. "The entire shift was rather uneventful, honestly, and for the most part, it was a shockingly safe day in Boston."

Her face began to relax.

I certainly hadn't missed how tense it looked.

"And it was a sunny day," she said.

I nodded. "I'm thankful for that." I took another sip, hoping I'd satisfied her enough that she would change the topic.

"I have news."

Relieved that I'd gotten my wish, I reached forward and grabbed a cube of cheese and a slice of prosciutto. "Oh, yeah? What kind of news?"

"I picked a man."

"What?" I said, chewing the bite that was in my mouth. "You already have a man, so why in the hell would you be looking for another one?"

"He's not for me. He's for you."

I shook my head. "Oh no."

"You know I've been dying to set you up with one of the art directors in my office, and now, it's finally time. Don't think I forgot the promise you made me."

Three months and one week ago, Rose had asked if she could set me up.

I'd told her I would consider it in three months.

She had been smart not to ask me last week.

She was even smarter to ask me now.

I set down the almost-empty glass I hadn't realized I'd been holding.

Just as I was about to respond, she said, "I'm not asking you to get serious with the guy. I just want you to meet him for dinner. The same thing we're doing right now. If there's chemistry, pursue him. If there isn't, then at least you tried."

"You really want to get me laid, don't you?"

"Is that a bad thing?"

I opened my mouth and then instantly closed it. I needed to

think about what I was going to say before something unforgettable came tumbling out of it. "No, I suppose it's not."

"Good." She grinned. "Then, let me get you laid."

I didn't know if I'd actually go on the date with the art director. But, to avoid one of Rose's talks, I smiled and made sure my tone was convincing when I said, "I can hardly wait."

TWO

DYLAN

THE FIRST TIME I had seen Alix Rayne, she had been walking into the restaurant I was dining at. She was there with a girl, who I later learned was Rose, her best friend. I was there with another woman.

I didn't mean to watch Alix move across the room. My date just wasn't holding my attention.

And, because I was used to taking in my surroundings, my peripheral vision more sensitive than most, once Alix entered from my direct right, I couldn't take my eyes off her.

She was absolutely fucking gorgeous.

Both women landed at a table less than ten yards from mine.

Alix sat, facing me.

Then, she laughed at something Rose had said and glanced down at the wine menu.

"Dylan?" my date said.

I turned my head, staring at her now but listening for sounds coming from the other table. "Yeah?"

"Didn't you want to order some wine with dinner? I think it should be here soon."

I didn't want to be rude, but I no longer wanted to have dinner with her.

Not even if that meant a guaranteed blow job in the backseat while my driver took her home.

I wanted to be with the beautiful woman at the other table. The one with long chocolate-colored hair and a curvy waist and lips that naturally were pouty and pale pink.

Just as I was about to respond, a vibration came from the inside of my jacket. I reached into my pocket and took out my cell. When I saw the name on the screen, I said to my date, "I have to take this." My finger swiped the phone, and I held it up to my ear, "Yes?"

"I have a situation," my assistant said.

"Talk."

"One of the pilots showed up, under the influence. He's been sent home, and boarding has been delayed. The plane is scheduled to leave Logan International Airport in thirty minutes. I've contacted all of the other pilots in the area, and none are available. How would you like to proceed?"

"Where's it going?"

"Las Vegas."

She wanted to know if I would fly the plane or if she should book the passengers a commercial flight and issue them a credit for the inconvenience.

My customers used my airline for many reasons.

One of those was that we always got them into the air, and it was never on a commercial vessel.

We figured it out.

No matter what that looked like.

Therefore, she knew my answer before I said, "I'll be there in thirty minutes."

"I'll let the airport know."

I put the phone into my jacket and reached into my back

pocket for my wallet. I took out three one-hundred-dollar bills, knowing that was more than enough to cover everything we had ordered, and set them on the table. "I have to go."

"What? Seriously?"

I got up from the table and moved around to her chair. I put my hand on her shoulder and said, "Stay. Enjoy yourself. Eat your meal ... and mine. If you want. It was nice meeting you ..." I stopped and cleared my throat, trying to remember her name. It didn't come to me, and I had nothing left to say, so I walked away.

But I didn't leave the restaurant.

I went to Alix's table, stood right at her side, and put my back toward my date. "Excuse me," I said.

Rose was already looking at me.

Not Alix.

I had to wait for her to slowly turn to me, her gaze gradually lifting until it reached my face. "Hi."

"I want to give you something."

She smiled out of nervousness. "Okay."

"Give me your hand."

"She's not giving you anything until I know what this is about," Rose said.

The dynamics of their friendship were defined in that moment.

So were their personalities.

I glanced at Rose. "What I'm about to give her isn't going to hurt her."

"I don't know that."

I reached into my back pocket again, took out my wallet, and gave it to her. "You have everything in there—my ID, pilot's license, credit cards, debit card, and over a thousand in cash. If something happens to her, you can hand it over to the police. Except for the cash; you keep that."

She looked up from her palm where it was all resting and eventually said, "Fair enough."

My stare returned to Alix. "Please give me your hand."

She lifted it off her lap, and as it moved through the air, I caught it and flipped her hand around. As I held her palm face up, I took a pen out of my jacket and pressed it against her skin, running the tip length-wise.

When I finally released her, she looked at it to see what I had written. "Your phone number?"

I nodded.

"You could have typed it into my cell."

"That's too impersonal."

"And writing on my hand isn't?"

Out of all the questions, she'd asked that one.

"I got to touch you," I said, my tongue circling the corner of my lip from the memory of what she had felt like. "And then I got to watch and feel the way you responded to me."

She searched my eyes, her cheeks beginning to redden. "I could be married."

I didn't care if she was.

That was how strongly I felt for this girl after being in her presence for only a minute.

"Then, don't call me. Or do. The decision is up to you."

When I took a few steps toward Rose, Alix said, "Where are you going?"

I waited for Rose to put my wallet on top of my hand before I said, "The airport. I have a plane to fly."

"You're a pilot." She didn't say it as though she were questioning me. She said it like she was storing the information, cementing it in her brain even though this was the second time I'd told her.

"I'm many things," I answered, and then I left the restaurant.

Thirty-eight minutes later, I was in the air.

13

THREE

ALIX

PRESENT DAY

MY TOWNHOUSE WAS ONLY six blocks from the restaurant—too close to get a car service, just far enough away to fill my body with fresh air. So, after having dinner with Rose, I walked home, taking in the smells and sounds and sights of the city.

Boston was never quiet.

I appreciated that.

Silence was like moisture; it created an environment that allowed things to grow. Fester. Eat into the walls and foundation.

I didn't want to give my thoughts that kind of space and freedom inside my brain. I knew they'd never go away, but I wanted them to stay dormant for the rest of my life.

Therefore, I preferred the loudness, especially when it seeped through the windows of my brownstone and padded the rooms with noise.

There seemed to be an extra dose of it this evening, which excited me as I continued to head home. When I turned onto my block, my speed increased, and I hurried up the five steps.

I unlocked the door.

Keys were placed in a bowl on a table in the entryway, and I set my bag on the closest barstool in the kitchen.

There was a note from Dylan on the counter.

I smiled as I read it and grabbed the bottle of red that was next to it. When my eyes landed on the last word, I filled a glass and carried it into the bedroom.

My jewelry was dumped in a drawer on the right side of the closet, my clothes in the hamper, my shoes wherever they landed on the floor.

Without stopping in the bathroom to brush my teeth or wash off my makeup, I brought the wine over to the bed, and I climbed in. Once I was settled, I reached toward the tablet on the night-stand, pressing the button that flipped off the lights and another that turned on the TV.

HGTV.

That was all I ever watched.

While I was still sitting up, I took a few sips of wine, my lower body sinking into the mattress, my muscles slowly starting to relax. Once the feeling moved toward my center, I set the glass next to the tablet and slid until my head was nestled into the fluffy down of the pillow.

I tugged the blanket up to my neck, and the warmth of the wine began to move to my face.

My eyes closed.

I rolled onto my stomach, the coolness of the top sheet now resting over my bare ass.

Just as I was hugging a pillow against my side, I heard him.

I smiled again.

And then I exhaled a long, deep sigh. "I've missed you, Dylan," I whispered.

"I've missed you."

He was here.

With me.

That was the only thing I wanted.

"I can't stop thinking about you," he added.

That made me shiver.

Even harder.

I felt movement, and the blanket shifted. Then, suddenly, he was on top of me.

His smell.

His touch.

His presence.

I loved all of it.

While I stayed on my stomach, his mouth traveled down my back, peppering my spine with kisses. It forced my lips to spread almost as wide as my legs.

"You're so fucking beautiful, Alix."

Oh God.

My arm shot out from under the pillow, and it feathered down the front of me until two of my fingertips were pressed against my clit. "I want you," I moaned.

My hips shifted higher to give him more access, his tip easily finding my wetness.

He growled in my ear, and then I heard, "You're going to get all of me."

I swallowed.

And then I gasped as his long thickness thrust deep inside me.

It was perfection.

So was the sensation that consumed my entire body, the tingles that spread to each of my limbs.

Emotion burned my chest.

And, with each stroke, my pussy pulsed even more.

"I love you," I breathed.

It was true.

I loved him more than anything in this entire world.

He knew that.

I constantly told him.

"I love you, too, Alix."

He always made his feelings extremely clear, and they were as strong as mine.

The prickling in my navel moved higher, the pulsing in my clit began to really throb.

My hair was pulled, and my face came out of the pillow; warm air surrounded it, and I felt his kisses on my neck and along my shoulder and all the way up my cheek.

It wasn't just the intimacy I craved.

It was the affection, too.

And the build.

I was there.

So close.

I tilted my hips up, rocking them back and forth as the orgasm began to burst through me. "Dylan!" I shouted.

"Come for me."

His demand was so incredibly sexy.

And it was what I needed to take me over that final edge.

While I moaned his name, his strokes turned even deeper and harder than before, and then he switched to short plunges until everything inside me and around me went completely still.

"Your pussy will always be mine," I heard him say before he slid out.

My hair was released, my face slowly pressed into the pillow.

"Yours," I uttered so softly.

His warmth moved across my back once again before the blanket was tucked over me, and I heard, "Good night, Alix," spoken in his low, growly voice.

I felt his hand surround mine.

My eyes remained shut.

I took a breath.

And I whispered, "I'm so happy you came home tonight," before I fell asleep.

Light from the open blinds trickled into the bedroom, shining directly on my face, waking me from the deepest of sleep. As my eyes opened, the sun burned my lids, so I quickly shielded them with the back of my hand.

I was still on my stomach.

I'd slept all night in the same position.

Rotating to my back, I gradually let in more of the light until I could keep both eyes open.

The first thing I saw was the empty spot beside me on the bed.

A coldness slipped inside my body.

I lifted the blanket, pulled it over my head, and tucked myself in a ball.

I hugged two pillows against my chest.

I squeezed them with all my strength.

My face dropped into the top of one.

My mouth opened.

I filled my lungs.

My jaw widened as far as it would go.

My eyes squinted shut.

And then I screamed.

This one didn't have any sound.

This one was silent.

Still, my body shook as it all came out of me.

And it continued until there wasn't any air left.

That was when I stilled.

When I shut my mouth.

When I waited for something to happen.

When I waited to feel different.

But nothing happened.

Nothing felt different.

So, I peeked out of the comforter to reach the tablet, hitting the button that would close the blinds. Once they were drawn, I wrapped the blanket over the top of my head.

I was in complete darkness.

That was where I belonged.

And that was where I stayed.

FOUR

ALIX

PRESENT DAY

Unknown: Hey, it's Peter. I work with Rose. Hopefully, she told you I'd be reaching out.
Me: Hi, Peter. Yes, she told me.
Peter: Are you free this weekend? Maybe we could do dinner or something?
Me: Yeah, that works.
Peter: How about Madison's? Saturday at 8:00?
Me: I'll see you there.

FIVE

DYLAN

SHE'D CALLED.

It had taken her three weeks and two days, but at last, she'd finally reached out.

It'd happened just as I was stepping out of a meeting with a company that was trying to sell me leather. It would be used to reupholster the seats and couches for my entire fleet of planes.

All forty-three of them.

I was a few paces past the conference room on the way to my office when my cell rang. The screen showed a number that began with Maine's only area code.

I shut my door, held the phone to my ear, and said, "Dylan Cole."

"So, that's your name."

I smiled as I walked to my desk.

I received over fifty calls a day.

But, before I'd answered, something had told me it was her—a woman whose name I still didn't know.

"Now that you know mine, what's yours?"

"Alix Rayne."

Alix.

I liked the sound of that.

I also liked how sexy her voice was on the phone.

"You don't do anything on a whim, do you, Alix?"

"Why do you say that?"

I waved off my assistant as she popped her head in, and I swiveled the chair around to face the wall of windows. "Most people send a text the next day, two days max. Or they scrub off the ink with no intention of ever calling. But they don't usually keep the number and wait three weeks to use it."

"I was moving. That's why I didn't phone you sooner."

I grabbed a stress ball off my desk. I threw it into the air, caught it, and tossed it right back up. "My best friend owns a moving company. I could have had you relocated and unpacked within a few hours."

"I wouldn't have accepted your offer, Dylan. My roommates and I are more than capable of handling it."

I shifted in my seat as the ball went wide to the left, and I threw it high. "It sounds like you have more than one."

"I have three."

"Three?" I said, laughing.

I hadn't lived with that many people since college, and that was ten years ago.

I wasn't sure how old Alix was. I guessed mid-twenties, which meant she should be well past the sorority stage of her life.

"Two of the guys at the station were looking for roommates. Rose and I were, too, so we moved in with them."

"Rose is?"

"The girl I was eating dinner with the night I met you."

Now, I was just intrigued.

"And what station are you referring to?"

"Engine thirty-three, ladder fifteen—the firehouse on Boylston Street."

22

Since I hadn't known her name until a few seconds ago, I hadn't been able to look Alix up, so I didn't know anything about her.

Now that I was getting a taste, I wanted more.

"Do you work there?"

"Yes, I'm a paramedic."

A marketing executive, a real estate agent, the owner of an art gallery, I could picture. But Alix dressed in a uniform, straddling someone on a gurney while performing CPR, I could not.

That didn't mean I hated the image in my mind.

I liked it.

A hell of a lot.

She was a first responder, and there wasn't anything more honorable than that.

Especially in a city as challenging as Boston.

"I'm impressed," I said.

"Thank you."

"Tell me something, Alix. Why would a woman like yourself have three roommates?"

"Like myself?"

I rolled the ball over the armrest of the chair. "Strong, independent. Fearless."

She stayed quiet for a few seconds before she said, "My parents feel more comfortable when I live in a building that has a doorman. They've spent their whole lives in innocent ole Maine. The thought of me being in this big city terrifies them. And that's where my place has to be located because it's one of my job requirements. With those two expensive necessities, I'd be rent poor if I didn't have roommates."

I knew what city employees made.

My mother was one.

So, I understood Alix's situation.

"Where are you?" I asked.

"You mean, right this second?"

"Yes."

"I'm walking out of the firehouse, heading home."

I'd lived in Boston my entire life, so I knew the general area of where that firehouse was located. I just didn't know the cross street. "How far are you from Back Bay Station?"

"Maybe seven blocks or so."

"When you get there, take the orange line to Downtown Crossing. I'll be there when you walk outside."

"Wait. You want me to get on the train to meet you? Now?"

I looked at my computer, clicking on the calendar to bring up my schedule. It showed I had four more meetings today, one that started in fifteen minutes. Two of them were conference calls with the West Coast office, and in an hour, one was with the pilot who had received a one-month suspension for showing up drunk to the airport.

"Do it on a whim, Alix."

Several seconds passed before she said, "Okay, I'll see you there."

SIX

ALIX

PRESENT DAY

MADISON'S, the restaurant where I was meeting Peter, was only a few blocks from my townhouse, making it easy to walk there. As I put on my jacket, I wondered what Rose had told him about me and if he'd chosen to eat there because of how close it was to my place.

I had to ask her.

We were overdue for a chat anyway. I was supposed to call her when I got home from work today, but I had been too busy, getting ready.

So, once I shut the front door behind me, carefully walking down the steps, I took out my cell and pressed her name in my Contacts.

She answered after the first ring and said, "Girl, I was giving you five more minutes before I called you and chewed your ass out. You're going on a date tonight. How can we *not* talk first?"

"I know. I'm sorry."

"You're forgiven."

I laughed. "I need to clarify something really quick. This is not a date."

"What is it then?"

I thought about her question, trying to come up with the answer that had caused me to put on several different outfits before I settled on this one and spent a little extra time doing my makeup.

The truth was, "I honestly don't know."

"It doesn't need a label. You're going out; let's leave it at that. Tell me what you're wearing."

Even though I knew what was covering my body, I looked down as I passed a large group of men. "Skinny jeans, a light-weight sweater, and knee-high boots."

"Did you have a glass of wine before you left?"

I wondered if I would ever reach a point in my life when she stopped asking that question. "A half of a glass."

"Good," she responded. "I hoped you would celebrate even if I wasn't there to force you to."

This was another moment.

At least she believed it was one.

I didn't want to think too much about it, so I changed topics and said, "What are you and Terry doing tonight?"

Terry was Rose's fiancé. They'd started dating shortly after we all moved in together, which was about the same time I'd met Dylan. When things turned serious between Terry and Rose, they got their own place, and two firemen from a different station moved in with me.

A few months later, I'd left, too.

Just as I began to unzip that memory while Rose was telling me what their plans were for tonight, I heard a sound.

It was one I couldn't ignore.

One I'd been tuned in to for years.

It was the sound of someone who needed help.

My feet stopped, and I scanned the area in front of me and on both sides until I found the source. There were two men just steps inside the mouth of the alley up ahead. One was sitting on the ground, hunched forward. The other was hovering over him, trying to evoke a response.

It took less than a second to assess the situation.

My heart began to race, my hands trembling to the point where I almost dropped the phone.

The man kneeling was shaking the unconscious guy's shoulders.

There was still no reaction from him.

My experience told me he would only get worse without a medical intervention.

He needed an EMT, and then he needed to be brought to the hospital.

It was a process I was quite familiar with.

But, even if I wanted to help him, I didn't know if I could.

God, I needed to pull myself together.

I needed to slow down my breathing and stop my body from quivering.

To start, I blinked.

Hard.

And I saw that I was standing in the center of the sidewalk.

Frozen.

There were people moving by me in both directions.

I still had the phone pressed against my ear, and Rose was blabbing away.

I shook my head. I stared at the two men, and I forced myself to focus on what I needed to do.

"... and we'll order some sushi—"

"Rose, I have to go," I said, cutting her off.

I disconnected the call and filled my lungs with as much air as they could hold. Then, I willed my body to loosen enough that I could rush over to the entrance of the alley. When I got there, I said, "Do you need help?"

The guy who was kneeling quickly looked up at me. "Are you a doctor?"

There wasn't time to tell him about all the training I'd had. Instead, I slid in next to them and lowered myself until I was at their eye-level. "I'm someone who can help. What's his name?"

"Joe Marino."

I pressed my fingers against the side of Joe's wrist. "Joe?" I used a sharp, stern voice. "Joe, can you open your eyes and look at me?" His pulse was extremely slow. "What has he taken?"

"Just a lot of booze."

I pushed Joe's upper body until he was no longer slumped forward, and his back was resting against the building. Now that his head was lifted, I evaluated him again. His lips were beginning to turn blue. His cheeks were flushed, telling me his temperature was rising. I lifted his eyelids to see how his pupils would react to the flashlight on my phone. They were dilated.

"Are you sure that's all he's taken?" I asked.

Joe's jaw slacked, and I heard crackling coming from the back of his throat.

"His wife served him with divorce papers this morning. I guess it's possible he could have popped something before I met him at the bar. But, shit, I don't know."

I turned off the flashlight and brought up the keypad on my phone. "Who are you?"

"Smith Reid, his best friend."

"When was the last time you saw him conscious?"

I kept my eyes on Joe while Smith said, "Just a minute ago. We were in the bar, and I could tell it was time for him to go home. We made it through the door, and he fell on me. I carried him over here to check him out and see what the hell was going on. You showed up a few seconds later."

Without responding to Smith, I hit nine, one, one on my phone. Once the call was answered, I said, "I'm dispatcher eight, four, nine, nine, three, seven for Boston. I'm in an alleyway between Beacon and Fairfield Street with an unresponsive male, approximately thirty years of age, experiencing a slowed heart rate, dilated pupils, cyanosis, and a restricted airway. From my observation, he's showing visible signs of an overdose. Please send an EMT."

"I have an ambulance in route," the dispatcher replied. "ETA is three minutes. What's the male's name?"

"Joe Marino," I said into the phone. "He's here with his best friend, Smith Reid. There's full access to the alley, nothing blocking the entrance. Tell the paramedics to bring a stretcher."

"I'll let them know right now," she said. "Will you be staying with Smith and Joe until the paramedics arrive?"

"Yes."

"Then, you're free to end the call."

As soon as I slipped the phone into my bag, my eyes connected with Smith's. "Can you hold up his chin? If there's any liquid in his airway, we have to make sure he doesn't choke on it."

Smith moved closer to Joe's side and positioned a hand at the base of his neck with another at the back of his head. "How long until they arrive?"

"Around two minutes."

"Is he going to be all right?"

In training, I'd been taught to never answer questions like that. So, I kept my attention on Joe and said, "I really don't know."

With my hand now on his forehead, it felt warmer, and his skin was turning even clammier.

There was nothing I could do to treat him. I didn't have any medical equipment in my purse, no Narcan or fluids.

"Do you really think he's overdosing?"

There was so much concern in his voice. As I quickly glanced at him, there was just as much in his face.

"With no way to test him, I can't confirm what's happening inside his body. The only things I can confirm are his symptoms."

"And they're showing you that he's ..." His voice trailed off, and he lifted his hand from Joe's neck and ran it through his hair. "Jesus fucking Christ, Joe. Open your eyes and look at me, buddy." When Joe didn't respond, Smith put his hand on his friend's chest and shook it. "Open your goddamn eyes. I know you can hear me right now."

I didn't stop him because I didn't think movement would hurt Joe's condition.

"What the fuck did you take?" He got closer to Joe's face. "You didn't have to do this. We would have figured it out. I would have helped you; you know that."

Just as Joe's pulse slowed a little more, I heard the sound of the siren. By how loud it was, it couldn't have been more than a few blocks away.

"They're almost here," I said to Smith.

My fingers stayed on Joe's wrist, constantly monitoring his heart rate in case it lowered to where I needed to give him CPR. My eyes were glued to him, taking in the coloring of his skin, the movement in his face, every rise of his chest. And my ears were focused on the sounds that came from his mouth.

When the paramedics got out of the ambulance and approached us, I gave them Joe's pulse, and then I said to Smith, "Follow me."

"You're asking me to leave him?"

I looked over my shoulder. "I'm just asking you to step aside, so they have room to work on him. Once they get him in the ambulance, they'll let you on, and you can ride with them to the hospital."

Without another word, he got up and followed me to the sidewalk, moving several paces down the building.

The medics placed the stretcher outside the alley and took our places in front of Joe.

I turned around to face Smith. "Are you all right?"

His eyes didn't leave Joe, but from where we stood, we couldn't see much. "That's my best friend over there. I don't know if he's going to make it. Fuck no, I'm not okay."

There was nothing I could say to assure him that Joe would make a full recovery. It just depended on what his vitals showed, how his body continued to respond, how the EMTs medically treated him on the way to the hospital.

What I knew was, every second Joe went untreated, it decreased his percentage of survival.

The medics working on him knew that, too.

"Let's wait over here," I said to Smith and led him to the side of the ambulance.

A crowd had started to form by the alley. I didn't want Smith to get forgotten once they had Joe on the stretcher.

"They need to fucking hurry up," Smith said. His arms were crossed over his chest, his breathing so much more rapid than his best friend's.

"They're good at what they do," I assured him.

Boston only hired the best, so he didn't have to worry about that.

He took a few steps forward and the same amount back. His hand shifted from his bicep to his hair to cupping the open door of the ambulance.

Since I still wasn't able to see much of Joe, I took the opportunity to evaluate Smith, something I still hadn't done yet.

The muscles in his jaw were tensing.

He was smashing his lips together, rubbing them against each other.

His Adam's apple bobbed as he swallowed.

But it was his expression I understood the most.

The pain, the helplessness.

It filled his eyes.

"Is there anything I can do to help you?"

He stopped pacing and glanced at me, but our eyes only connected for a second because, suddenly, there was movement in the alley. The medics were putting Joe on the stretcher, buckling him in and rolling him toward us.

"This is Smith Reid," I said to the paramedics, pointing at him. "He is Joe's best friend. He'll be riding with you to the hospital."

"No problem," one of the medics said as they got ready to lift the stretcher inside.

When Smith's eyes landed on me again, I said, "Good luck."

I didn't wait for him to respond.

I just immediately walked away and didn't stop until I saw the familiar row of dark red brick and the five front steps that led up to my townhouse.

I unlocked the door.

Keys were placed in a bowl on the table in the entryway, and I set my bag on a barstool in the kitchen.

I grabbed the bottle of red and carried it along with my phone into the bedroom. As I dumped my jewelry in a drawer on the right side of the closet, I saw Dylan's handwritten note on the bottom shelf next to a pair of heels.

He always left them in the craziest spots.

I read his words.

I love you, too, I thought as I stripped off my clothes and dropped them in the hamper, my boots staying wherever they fell.

Keeping my makeup on, not even brushing my teeth, I carried the wine and my cell over to the bed, and I climbed in. Once I got comfortable and had several swigs of the red down my throat, I looked at the texts that were filling my screen.

Rose: *Why did you hang up so quickly? Is everything okay?*
Rose: *Why aren't you texting me back?*
Rose: *Peter said you haven't shown up to the restaurant. I'm*
freaking out right now, Alix. Where are you?
Rose: *CALL ME.*

I would call her once I caught my breath.

Once I replayed everything that had just happened and I got it settled in my mind.

Because what had just gone down was a moment.

One that needed to be celebrated.

I would get there.

It was just going to take me more than two seconds.

SEVEN

DYLAN

THREE YEARS AND ONE MONTH AGO

ALIX WALKED up the stairs to exit the Downtown Crossing station and stepped onto Summer Street. She looked to her right and then slowly turned toward her left.

That was where I was standing.

Fifteen feet away.

Our eyes locked.

Her smile pounded my chest like a goddamn mallet.

In that moment, everything made sense.

Answers filled my head.

All of them had to do with her.

Alix Rayne.

The woman who was about to change my whole fucking life.

EIGHT
ALIX
PRESENT DAY

WITHIN THIRTEEN MINUTES of entering my townhouse, I was in bed. Naked. The blanket pulled up to my neck, a bottle of wine in my hand that I rested on top of the mattress.

HGTV was playing on the television.

Muted.

Both bedside table lamps were on.

In the last several seconds, I'd played and processed my encounter with Smith and Joe.

I'd celebrated the moment internally.

It was another milestone after all.

And it had been a big one.

Now, it was time to call Rose, whose panicked texts I still hadn't replied to.

I opened my call log, found her name, and pressed it.

"Alix, are you okay?"

I shouldn't have waited so long to call.

I should have phoned her when I'd gotten inside my townhouse.

But I couldn't have.

My return couldn't have gone in that order.

I'd had to unlock the door first, then drop the keys and my bag, grab the wine, get undressed, and climb into bed.

"Yes," I promised. "I'm fine."

She sighed, and I could tell how relieved she was. "What the hell happened that caused you to hang up, not return my texts, and not show up to dinner?"

Dinner.

Shit, I'd forgotten all about it.

"Please apologize to Peter for me."

I had his number.

I never planned on using it again.

"Alix, seriously, start talking."

My stare dropped to the bed, to the empty spot that was just to the right of me.

The spot Dylan should be lying on.

He should have his shirt off, wearing a sexy pair of boxer briefs. The blanket low on his waist, his hands crossed over his abs.

He had no idea how badly I needed him to come home tonight.

Or maybe he did.

"On the way to the restaurant, I came across two men in an alley," I confessed. "One of them needed help. I'm almost positive he was overdosing."

"Oh God, Alix."

"I stopped and helped them, and then I left."

"You're home now?"

"Yes." I tightened my grip on the bottle, lifting it to my lips, chugging down several mouthfuls. "Ask me if I'm celebrating."

"Are you?"

"I skipped the glass and went straight for the bottle."

"I'm proud of you, babe." She was silent for several seconds. "Do you want to talk about it?"

"No." And, because I knew her so well, I added, "I'm okay, I promise."

"How about I come over and sleep at your place tonight?"

This wasn't the first time she'd offered to do that.

"No, I'm really all right. I'm just going to go to bed."

"Understandable." The concern in her voice was gone. "I'm going to call you in the morning."

"I figured," I said. "Good night."

I hung up and placed the phone on the nightstand, setting the wine next to it. I then hit the screen of the tablet to turn off the lights and lifted the blanket up to my nose, rolling until I faced Dylan's side of the bed.

I was just about to shift positions again when I heard him.

Excitement immediately filled me.

As I waited for him to come into the bedroom, my lids squeezed closed, my body tensing up with anticipation.

He was giving me what I needed.

I wondered if he knew that.

The noises got louder.

And then, slowly, I felt movement and a wave of warmth as he got into bed behind me.

"You're here." I took a breath.

"Yes."

"I didn't think you'd come."

Guilt began to pound through my chest.

I'd left the house to go on a date.

With Peter.

Because Rose wanted me to get laid.

But she didn't know about Dylan's visits.

I couldn't tell her about them either.

"Tonight was so hard," I whispered, not knowing why those

37

words had left my mouth. "I was on my way out and ..." I paused as I felt his lips touch the top of my shoulder. "There was a man who needed my help."

I knew why he wasn't saying much.

I just wished he wasn't being so quiet.

"I didn't work on him," I continued. "But I assessed him and I called for help and ..."

The rest didn't matter.

I'd covered the points that had been cause for celebration.

I smashed my lids together even harder as I waited for him to tell me he was proud, that I'd done a good job—things that would mean more to me than anything.

But all I got was a hug.

A long one.

One that I felt around my whole body.

He always knew what I really needed.

And an embrace was certainly it.

"Please stay," I said softly.

There were several moments of silence before I felt movement, and he was pushing himself off the bed.

"I can't," was all I heard.

Some nights, he didn't leave.

Tonight just wasn't one.

"Dylan, I love you."

I didn't get a response, so I looked over my shoulder. He wasn't in here, and the bedroom door was closed.

He was gone.

NINE

DYLAN

THREE YEARS AND ONE MONTH AGO

"HI," Alix said as she moved across the sidewalk. She closed the gap between us and stopped when she was about a foot away.

She was still dressed in her uniform—a white button-down and khakis and large black boots.

Somehow, she made it look sexy.

"You're here."

She glanced behind her at the stairs she had just climbed, and then her stare slowly returned to me. "I'm a little shocked, honestly."

I leaned my side into the brick exterior of the train station. "Why?"

She gazed up at me through her lashes.

She was shy.

That was something I'd noticed at the restaurant. I just hadn't realized how reserved she really was.

"Well, when I called, I didn't think you'd answer, so I just planned on leaving a message." Her voice was soft.

She needed to understand something, and because I was

more forward than her, I said, "Listen to me, Alix. You can always say no to me."

"I'm not sure I can."

As I looked into her eyes, the truth behind that statement revealed itself to me.

She felt the same way I did.

I didn't know what to call it.

I couldn't even describe it.

But it was something.

I'd known that from the moment I stood next to her at the restaurant.

Even more so when I wrote my number on her hand.

And, now, the feeling was even more intense than ever.

Enough that I needed to start walking or my fucking hands were going to reach for her.

I couldn't let that happen yet.

"Follow me." My hand went to her shoulder, moving her closer, before I led her toward State Street.

Just as I took a step, I heard, "Wait."

I glanced at my side, our eyes locking.

"I need to know something first."

"What?"

"Is she still in the picture?"

She.

The girl I had been with that night.

It was a fair question.

"She's long gone." My lids narrowed as I took her in. "Let me assure you of something, Alix. Had my assistant not called, dragging me away from that dinner, I still would have ended up at your table; it just might have taken me a few minutes longer to get there."

Her cheeks flushed.

Her body seemed even tenser than before.

"You don't need to charm me."

I laughed.

I wasn't sure how men typically acted around her. With how gorgeous she was, I assumed they hit on her all the time.

That wasn't what I was doing.

"I'm just telling you the truth." Instead of waiting for her to respond, I looked straight ahead and began to walk, bringing her over the cobblestones toward Quincy Market. Once we were well past the train station, I asked, "Are you hungry?"

She shrugged. "I'm the kind of girl who can always eat."

"That's the kind of girl I like."

Her cheeks flushed again.

It was a sight I'd never grow tired of.

"I'm about to feed you the best lunch you've ever had in Boston." Rather than going into Quincy Market, I took her around the side of the building to the last pushcart in the row and stood with her in the short line.

"I feel like you really believe that." She was nervous, fidgeting with her hands, shifting her weight between her feet.

"When it comes to food, I'm an expert," I told her. "Trust me."

A smile was the only response I got.

But what I liked was that there was nothing simple about that movement of her lips. Her grin traveled as high as her eyes, and it changed the color in her cheeks and caused a tiny twitch in her nose.

It was all so genuine.

When we reached the front of the line and it was my turn to order, I asked for two extra-crispy gyros.

The preparation started with tzatziki sauce slathered onto the pitas, followed by an assembly line of vegetables and meat, which had been stuck back on the grill to cook the way I'd requested.

Once both were wrapped in foil and paid for, I said to Alix, "One more stop," and I backtracked four carts.

There, I ordered fries from a vendor who sliced the potatoes right in front of us and dropped them into a fryer. When they were golden brown and placed in a large bowl, I handed him some cash and went over to the condiments.

"Vinegar?" Alix said as I lifted the bottle.

I looked at her. "You've never had it on your fries?"

She shook her head, and I glanced back down, drizzling the vinegar over the whole bowl, adding in some salt and a large squirt of ketchup.

"Once you have them like this, you'll never eat them any other way."

I moved us over to a vacant bench, and as I put the fries between us, my hand gently grazed the outer edge of her thigh. The small gasp she made was just the sound I'd wanted to hear.

I pulled my fingers away and said, "Go ahead; try them."

She wasn't careful about the way she dipped one into the pool of ketchup or how she popped it into her mouth. She also wasn't afraid to get her fingers dirty.

I liked that.

"Wow." She chewed and took another fry, drowning it in ketchup first. "These really are the best I've ever had."

"I know." I handed her a gyro and bit off the corner of mine, watching as she eventually did the same to hers. "What do you think?"

"Holy shit," she said as she swallowed.

I smiled at her response and at the way she was eyeing the sandwich.

"This is incredible, Dylan." She spoke behind her hand, so I couldn't see the sauce that I knew was on her lips.

It was fucking adorable.

She grabbed several more fries and added, "I'm starting to believe you're the expert you said you were."

"It only gets better."

"The food?"

"All of it."

It was a promise.

One I intended on keeping.

As she processed what I'd just told her, I went over to one of the carts and grabbed some extra napkins, handing her several as I returned to the bench.

"Why don't you tell me about you?" she said as I sat back down.

Her shyness was resurfacing, and she wanted the attention off of her.

I wiped my mouth and held the gyro close to my lap. "You know I'm a pilot. What you don't know is, I own a private airline."

"Wow." Shock registered on her face even though half of it was hidden behind a handful of napkins.

"I've been in the air since I was a kid," I told her. "My father was a pilot and my grandfather, too, so it's in my blood. But I enjoy the business side just as much as flying; therefore, I knew one over the other would never be enough."

"So, naturally, you went and opened your own airline. That makes perfect sense."

Her sarcasm made me laugh.

It sounded so hot, coming out of her.

So did the giggle.

God, that girl is fucking beautiful.

"None of it came easy," I told her. "It took years to build what I have now and a hell of a lot of people who believed in my dream and had the money to back it. Fortunately, Embassy Jets has done better than the investors and I projected."

43

She set down the gyro and ate several fries. "What about your family? Are they in Boston?"

"I have a sister in Seattle, and my parents are in Somerville, in the same house I grew up in. Dad's retired now. Mom, too. They play bridge every Tuesday. It's a whole lot of fucking normal."

She swallowed the fries. "Same—except I'm an only child, neither of my parents are pilots, and I grew up in southern Maine."

"Portland?"

"Falmouth."

"Even nicer," I said. I knew the area well, as I'd flown into Portland many times and checked out the surrounding cities. "There's a corner store in Falmouth. I can't remember the name, but it has the best whoopie pies I've ever tasted."

"Nina's Variety, and you're right; they do."

Her lips parted as she lifted the gyro and took a bite.

A mouthful so big, it made me proud of her.

Alix was cool.

Much more than just a pretty face.

This girl had substance.

She had a story.

It was one I wanted to hear.

And one I wanted to be a part of.

"I want to do this again," I said.

"Me, too."

Once I got up, I reached down to help her stand. "You ready for dessert?"

She showed me her sandwich, which she'd only eaten half of. "I don't think I can fit in another bite."

"Find the room." I tossed her gyro into a trash bin along with the rest of mine and the empty bowl of fries. Then, I placed my hand on her lower back and led her toward the entrance of

Quincy Market. "I'm about to feed you some chocolate cake that will blow your mind."

Her laugh was sweet this time. "I believe you."

"You do like chocolate, don't you?" I opened the door for her to enter, and I walked in behind her. It was then that I realized I hadn't asked if she liked gyros or the vegetables they'd put on her sandwich or even French fries.

"It's my favorite," she replied.

Damn it.

I liked her even more now.

TEN

ALIX

PRESENT DAY

I ARRIVED at the police headquarters several minutes before my shift started and went straight to my desk, immediately logging into the system.

I hadn't come early to pick up overtime. I had come to read the notes the paramedics had left in Joe's file.

Regardless of what they said, I wouldn't change the way I'd handled things last night.

It was a moment.

One I'd celebrated.

But I needed to know if the paramedics agreed with my assessment, so I typed Joe's name into the search bar and watched his chart load. I skimmed all the stats the medics had entered— visible symptoms, vitals, the medication that had been administered.

They'd treated him for an overdose.

When they'd dropped him off at the hospital, he'd been alive and semi-responsive. I didn't have access to whatever had happened once he was there.

But what I had come to see was if their evaluation matched

mine.

And it did.

I'd done everything right.

I found myself taking a deep breath, my lungs feeling looser than they had all day. Air began to pass through even easier as I reread their notes a second and third time, finally comfortable enough to exit his chart.

I still had a few minutes before I needed to clock in, but I did anyway, and I put on the headset. Then, I clicked the screen that allowed me to answer inbound calls, and one came through almost immediately.

"Nine-one-one, what's your emergency?" I said.

And then it was back.

The ritual.

Inhaling wasn't so easy anymore.

My thumb tapped the space bar.

My body tensed.

My toes ground into the bottom of my shoes.

"My husband!" an older woman shouted into the phone. "I think he's having a heart attack."

I relaxed again, knowing that feeling would be brief and that I'd be repeating this process every few minutes for the next eight hours.

Tonight was a full moon.

The city would be even wilder.

Call counts would double.

Non-emergencies would turn life-threatening.

A shiver passed through me as I responded, "Help is on the way, ma'am." I sucked in some air. "What's your name, please?"

As she answered, I quickly glanced out the window, seeing the last speck of daylight.

It had been a sunny day.

I couldn't be more grateful for that.

ELEVEN

ALIX

PRESENT DAY

I WASN'T sure what time it was when I opened my eyes.

It didn't really matter.

Sun was coming through the blinds in the bedroom, and I could feel it on my face.

It was the perfect way to wake up after last night, one of the most draining shifts I'd ever worked.

My chest was tight from all the times it had been hard to take a breath.

The side of my thumb was raw from continuously tapping it on the space bar.

My muscles were sore from tensing them.

My toes ached from grinding them into the bottom of my shoes.

And my heart throbbed as I looked over at the other side of the bed.

There was no indent in the pillow. The comforter was still pulled up to the top.

He hadn't come home.

Goddamn it.

I grabbed his pillow and flung it across the room.

I needed him here.

He knew that.

It killed me every time he didn't show up.

I pushed myself higher in the bed, and my back slammed against the headboard. I reached for my phone, and just as I was about to open my Contacts and make a call, my thumb accidentally hit an app.

Pictures began to fill my screen.

So did notifications.

A few hundred of them.

Some were likes. The rest were emojis.

All were in response to the photo I'd posted earlier today.

During my walk home from the train station, I'd come across a rainbow made of chalk that a child had drawn on the sidewalk. As I had snapped a shot of it, the sun had shone over my hand and the phone, creating a shadow of my body behind the picture.

My followers knew all about sunny days.

I'd been sharing them more often.

But none had ever included a rainbow.

I scrolled through the comments under the picture and saw one from Rose.

It was a picture of a fist.

A moment.

She was right.

I filled my lungs, my chest almost feeling bruised, and I pressed an icon on the bottom of the screen. I wasn't sure what made me do it, but I typed *Smith Reid,* and I hit Search.

Only a handful of matches came up.

The first was a business account with a photo of him dressed in a suit. I clicked on the profile and learned he was a divorce attorney with a law firm in Downtown Crossing.

I knew the location well.

Dylan's office was a few buildings over.

I backed out and clicked on the second listing, which was Smith's personal profile. Even though I was a little hazy on what he and Joe looked like, I didn't remember Smith being so handsome.

But he was and extremely easy to stare at.

His features were sharp and rich.

His smile was inviting.

He had a warmth to him where Dylan was so cold.

I focused on the pictures, and what I learned within the first several rows were that Smith was active and outdoorsy.

He biked.

Ran.

And he ate.

There were photos of food from restaurants all over the city.

The more I continued to explore, I saw shots that he'd taken from different spots around the world.

Japan.

Dubai.

Alaska.

Peru.

I scrolled through more.

Two years back.

Three.

Smith's life was fascinating.

He didn't waste a second.

He didn't live with regret.

He just lived.

And he lived hard.

We certainly didn't have that in common.

When I reached the end, I worked my way back to the last shot he'd posted.

It was of him and Joe.

At the bar.

The night I had found them in the alley.

I checked the comments. There was nothing in there that updated me on Joe's status.

I had to know.

So, I tapped Smith's profile and clicked Send Message, and then I started to type.

Me: Hi, Smith. I'm Alix Rayne. We met last night in the alley. Anyway, I just wanted to see how you and Joe are doing.

In all the years I'd worked for the city, I'd never followed up with anyone before.

It wasn't that I didn't care.

If anything, I cared too much. That was why I'd chosen this field.

It just wasn't appropriate to reach out.

This situation was no different.

But it was.

Because I hadn't been on the other end of the phone.

Because I had found them and offered help.

I set my cell on my lap and reached for the tablet on the nightstand.

The blinds fully opened after I pressed a button, and the TV turned on.

HGTV.

The show was about designing a new master bathroom.

Mindless.

Just the way I liked it.

I watched it for only a few seconds before a notification came across the screen of my phone.

Smith had replied.

Smith: Hey, Alix. Thanks for checking on us. Joe's still in the hospital. If he continues to show progress, the doctor says he'll be discharged in a few days.
Me: And you?

I shouldn't have written back.

I should have closed out the app and continued watching bathroom remodels.

But I remembered the look in Smith's eyes.

The pain, the helplessness.

Smith: I'm doing all right.
Me: I'm relieved to hear that—and about Joe, too.
Smith: You were correct about his condition. He overdosed.
Me: I'm just glad he's going to be okay.
Smith: I don't think I ever thanked you for what you did. If you hadn't come along, I don't know if Joe would still be alive. He knows that—I've told him about you—and he's grateful as hell.
Me: I'm happy I could help.

I set my phone back on my lap, and as I stared at the TV, I wondered if Smith would look at my pictures. If he'd want to know more about the person who'd assisted him in the alley.

There were only about twenty shots on my page.

They were all of sunny days.

That was the only reason I kept my profile public.

Smith: Joe isn't in a place where he can thank you appropriately, but I can, and I'd like to. How about dinner? You pick the spot, and I'll be there.

I finished reading his message and set my cell on the nightstand. I pressed the different buttons on the tablet that would shut the blinds and turn off the TV. Then, I tucked the blanket over my head while I tightened my body into a ball.

Even though it was dark under the covers, I looked across the mattress at the unwrinkled bottom sheet, at the coldness that I would feel if I touched his spot.

What the fuck have I done?

TWELVE

DYLAN

ALIX and I were standing outside Quincy Market, holding our to-go boxes of chocolate cake, opened, with several forkfuls missing from each piece. I'd asked about her shift, which had started at midnight, and she was telling me about one of the calls she had been on. It involved an elderly couple, married for sixty-seven years. The husband had fallen down a short flight of stairs. Alix believed he had fractured his hip.

She stared at the cake as she spoke.

And I gazed at her, checking out the way she speared off another bite.

How she stuck the fork between her lips.

How the utensil came out of her mouth clean.

It was incredibly sexy.

So was she.

She didn't even have to try. It came natural to her.

As natural as her looks.

A beauty that went so deep, she didn't need makeup to enhance it.

She didn't wear much of it anyway. There wasn't anything on

her lips, no color on her lids, just thick lashes and some pink on her cheeks.

She had no idea how gorgeous she was.

If I told her, I was sure she wouldn't believe me.

Alix's confidence came when she talked about her job.

I could tell how much she loved it by the passion in her voice, by the way she described how she'd helped the old man.

What she did was something I hadn't been able to visualize at first. Now that I'd spent more time with her, it was all I could see.

Damn it, I wanted to touch her.

I'd kept my hands off of her while she was eating the gyro and fries.

But I didn't want to wait any longer.

Once she swallowed the mouthful, I said, "Alix ..."

I needed her eyes on me to see the way she would look at me, how she would respond to the sound of my voice.

That would determine if I could reach for her right now or if I'd have to wait.

Her stare slowly lifted and landed on mine.

Shyness was peeking through her expression.

Still, every sign was there—the desire in her glare, the increased breathing, the way her tongue was swiping across her lips. It wasn't frosting she was licking off because there wasn't any there.

I dropped the small box of cake on the ground.

She didn't watch it fall, but when she heard the sound, I saw the hunger in her grow.

I took a step.

She did, too, in the opposite direction at the same time she dropped her cake.

She said nothing as I continued to move toward her, backing her up to the side of the building until her body was pressed against it.

As I stood inches away, I lifted my hands to the top of her head where they pushed into the brick. "You can stop me."

Her voice was soft, not weak, as she looked up at me and said, "I'm not sure I can."

She'd responded the same way when I met her at the train station.

I had known what she meant then.

And again here, especially when her fingers went to my sides, holding them, using them to pull me toward her.

My head dipped.

My mouth sought hers.

Our lips touched.

A feeling came across my entire fucking body.

I couldn't let go of her.

That was why both palms dropped to her face, and I held her cheeks so tightly. Why, with every inhale, I kissed her even deeper. Why my hard-on was throbbing inside these suit pants.

She was the reason for every reaction.

My tongue found hers.

Her back arched, and her body leaned into mine.

My hand dropped to the side of her neck.

I took in her scent. It was a clean smell that had a hint of lemon.

I dragged my lips away but pressed my nose against hers.

I felt myself reaching for air, unable to get enough in.

She was doing the same.

"Fuck," I whispered.

I hadn't been prepared for that.

There was no way to summarize how the taste of Alix Rayne running through my body had become the most incredible sensation.

All I knew was that I needed more.

But more just couldn't happen here.

I pulled my face away, keeping one hand on her cheek, the other on her neck.

Her eyes gradually climbed from my chest until they locked with my stare.

I shouldn't take her home.

I should wait a few weeks, get to know her better, make sure she was comfortable with me.

I had all the time in the world.

But that wasn't me.

When I wanted something, I wanted it now.

"Do you want to get out of here?" I asked.

She nodded.

"I'm going to take you to my place."

She nodded again, and her hand tightened on my waist as though she were reminding me it was there.

I hadn't forgotten.

THIRTEEN

ALIX

PRESENT DAY

"SORRY," I said to Rose as I approached the small table she was sitting at, the restaurant she'd chosen for our happy hour. "I know I should have been here fifteen minutes ago."

It had taken some time to unravel from the ball of blanket I had tucked myself into. More time to get into the shower and find an outfit.

That was because Smith's last message wouldn't leave my mind.

It made me move slower.

And it ate at me until I replied.

While standing in my kitchen, just seconds after I slung my purse over my shoulder, I messaged Smith that I'd meet him for dinner. He answered with the restaurant he'd chosen, which was within walking distance to my place, and that he would make the reservation for eight o'clock.

Then, I headed over here, to the restaurant where Rose was waiting for me.

I had known responding to Smith would make me late.

I'd also known Rose wouldn't mind.

"Is everything okay?" she asked the second my ass hit the seat.

She was concerned.

I heard it.

I saw it.

She probably had reason to be.

I lifted the glass of wine she'd ordered for me and held it out toward her. She did the same with hers, meeting me in the middle of the table.

"We have a moment we need to toast to," I said.

"Oh, yeah?"

I clinked my glass against hers and took a sip, setting it down to loosen the lightweight scarf from my neck. "I'm going out on a date tomorrow night. Well, I shouldn't really call it a date. I'm just going out to dinner, so whatever that is, is what I'm doing."

She did an awful job at hiding her excitement as she leaned in to get closer, practically wiggling in her seat. "Tell me everything."

"He's the guy I helped in the alley. The best friend, not the patient."

She shook her head like she was trying to piece it together. "You guys swapped numbers?"

I wished I hadn't loosened the scarf so much because I wanted to hide my face beneath it. "I looked him up online and messaged him."

"Who are you? And what have you done with my best friend?"

I laughed because she was right.

Because the changes I was making felt good.

But then my voice turned serious when I said, "I just wanted to know if Joe was okay. That'd been weighing on me since it happened."

Her expression told me she wasn't surprised to hear this.

"I'm really proud of you for reaching out to him." When I didn't respond, she added, "But, like we did with Peter, let's not think too deep into what's happening. It's just dinner. If something goes down between you two, we'll celebrate another moment. If it doesn't, at least you took a chance." She wrapped her hand around her glass and brought it up to her lips. Once she set it down, the look on her face told me something big was coming. "Alix, we need to talk about Dylan."

And there it was.

I should have suspected this conversation was coming.

It had been a few weeks since she mentioned him.

She was overdue.

"No, we don't," I replied, trying to stop her before she took this any further.

"We can't keep avoiding this subject."

We had to—until I was able to tell her about Dylan coming home.

Until I could explain where things stood.

But I wasn't ready for that conversation yet.

"I just don't want to discuss him tonight."

She nodded, telling me she understood and that she wouldn't push me to chat about him tonight. Then, she glanced down at her menu. When she finally looked back up, there was a huge smile on her face. "Want to skip dinner and go straight to dessert?"

"More than anything."

She reached across the table and squeezed my hand. "That means we're going to need another bottle of wine."

"*Yesss*," I agreed.

She laughed.

I did, too.

This time felt even better.

When I saw the brick row of townhouses, mine being on the very end, I hurried down the rest of the sidewalk and up the front steps.

I unlocked the door.

Once I was inside, my keys were placed in the bowl in the entryway, and I set my bag on the closest barstool in the kitchen.

From there, I poured myself a glass of red and carried it into my bedroom.

I dropped my jewelry in a drawer on the right side of the closet, my clothes in the hamper, and my shoes on the floor by the rack of jeans.

There was a note from Dylan taped to the wall, next to his rack of belts.

I'LL TRY NOT TO BE LATE.
I LOVE YOU.

I didn't stop in the bathroom to brush my teeth or wash off my makeup. Instead, I brought the wine over to the bed, and I slid underneath the comforter. Once I was settled, I touched the screen of the tablet, hitting the buttons that flipped off the lights and turned on the TV.

HGTV.

Dream beach houses.

Perfect.

Still sitting up, I took several sips from the glass and eventually let my body sink into the mattress.

I was completely relaxed.

So much so that I set the glass by the tablet and adjusted my head over the pillow.

I brought the blanket up to my neck, and my body began to warm.

My eyes closed.

I was just turning to my side when I heard my bedroom door open.

I stayed where I was, frozen, and gasped, "You came?"

It didn't matter what the note had said.

I never assumed he would come.

I always just hoped.

"I'm so happy you're here," I added.

I heard, "Me, too," as he climbed into bed behind me.

That voice.

It was a sound I loved.

And with it came his touch, sending a fiery sensation down my back, covering my shoulders with the softest kisses.

He didn't have to question me.

He knew what I wanted.

He knew how to give it to me.

And, just like that, there was pressure around my nipple. A tugging, followed by a sharp pinch.

"My God," I groaned, my legs immediately spreading.

A finger went to my clit, running the length, turning in a circle when it reached the top.

"I want you," I breathed.

I barely had the last word out before he was plunging inside me.

The thrusts were deep and hard.

The movements so fast.

Every drive was emphasized when I felt the slap against the inside of my thighs.

My pussy contracted in response.

"Dylan," I gasped, the intensity building within me.

Fingertips traced my whole body. Breath was exhaled over my back.

"Fuuuck," was groaned near the side of my face.

His admission made me smile.

It lasted only a second before my lips puckered, and a moan poured out of them.

I was there.

It never took long with Dylan.

Just as I was about to tell him, "I know," was moaned in my ear.

The speed increased, my entire body tightened, and the first wave came over me.

My stomach shuddered.

A second wave pumped through me, and my sounds began to match his, telling me we were in the same place.

Both feeling the same things.

We were in this together because it was impossible for us to be apart.

I stilled when he pulled out.

I caught my breath.

I moved one arm underneath my pillow, and the other went closer to my face.

I didn't shift my body.

He was here.

We fit together.

This was the spot I'd fall asleep in.

I kept my eyes closed when I said, "Don't go. Please stay the night with me."

I waited for him to get off the bed.

For the loneliness to close in on me.

But what I felt in its place was the warmth from his arms as they circled around me, and then I heard the sound of, "Good night, Alix," floating in the air.

I was sleeping within a second.

Maybe two.

I woke to the sun touching my face.

Without my eyes opening, I quickly went to reach behind me, my hand moving out from under the pillow.

Before I even had my elbow bent, I heard, "I'm here."

Dylan had stayed the whole night.

My muscles relaxed.

My heart rate slowed.

I should have known the sunlight wasn't the only heat in this room.

It wasn't the only comfort either.

But, as I took it all in, as I thought about how perfectly this sunny day was starting, a feeling of dread dropped into my stomach.

It was hard to say.

Still, I had to get it out.

He had to hear it.

From me.

"I'm having dinner with another man tonight," I admitted. I ground my teeth together as I took several deep breaths. "Dylan, I want you to tell me not to go out with him."

My eyes squinted.

My chest pounded.

"Please," I begged. "Just say the words, and I'll stay home tonight."

I clung my hand around the blanket, the other twisting the edge of the fluffy pillow. "Dylan ..." I said so softly.

There was movement on the bed.

The air behind me suddenly turned to ice.

"Dylan, no."

He couldn't leave.

At least not without saying something.

But I heard his feet on the floor, and I knew that was exactly what he was doing.

"Please, Dylan. Don't go yet."

My body began to tense into a ball.

"Come back," I called.

The bedroom door opened.

Why did I tell him?

Why was I so honest?

Why didn't I just keep my mouth shut?

There was no reason I'd needed to tell him what I was doing with Smith.

I could have kept it in.

Lied.

I wasn't sure it would have even mattered.

"Dylan—" I cried out, cutting myself off when the bedroom door closed behind him.

He was gone.

He hadn't told me not to go.

He wouldn't.

I hated that more than anything.

I hated this feeling.

I hated what we had become.

To clear my head, I should climb out of bed, put some clothes on, walk down the five front steps, and spend the day outside. I should get coffee on Newbury Street and eat lunch in the Public Garden and shop for some new spring clothes at the Prudential Center.

But I didn't do any of that.

I reached for the tablet and pressed the button that closed the blinds, and I buried myself under the blanket.

I sucked in until my lungs felt like they were going to explode.

I opened my mouth.

And I screamed.

No sound came out.

It was a silent one.

But, in my head, it was the loudest noise I'd ever heard.

FOURTEEN

DYLAN

THREE YEARS AND ONE MONTH AGO

I WAS LYING on my left side, Alix was on her right, and we were facing each other, naked, in my bed. With my hand on her neck, I could feel the heat on her skin, the sweatiness. Her pulse hammering away under my fingers.

We had rushed back to my place from Quincy Market.

Once we arrived, that was when the hurrying stopped.

That was because I wanted to take my time with her body.

I tasted.

I nipped.

I licked, starting at the center of her ankles and then moving between her legs. I stayed there until she came, until she squirmed against my mouth, until I thought she was going to rip my hair out from pleasure. That was when I rose to her lips and pressed mine against them.

By then, my cock felt like it was going to fucking explode.

I didn't want her mouth on it.

I wanted her pussy.

Her wetness.

Her tightness.

The way it would squeeze my dick when she got off.

I'd felt all three.

Multiple times.

And, now, we were catching our breaths as we rested on top of my bed.

The little bit of makeup she'd had on earlier was gone. Her cheeks were flushed, her long hair a mess.

This was Alix.

Vulnerable.

Raw.

Perfect.

Not just for me, but in general.

She had a body that was even more beautiful out of clothes. A smile that hit me like a fist, shocking the hell out of me each time I saw it. A softness that was present long before I stripped off her uniform.

I took in the darkness of her eyes and skimmed her jaw with my thumb. "Are you hungry?"

"Hungry?" She laughed. "We just had lunch and chocolate cake."

That sound.

The lightheartedness of it.

It was something I could listen to every day.

"We're going to have dinner, too," I told her.

Her brows rose. "Tonight?"

I nodded, thinking of which restaurant I wanted to order from and how I would send my driver to pick it up.

"What if I already have plans?" she asked.

"Cancel them."

"Just like that?"

I stared into her eyes. "Yes, Alix, just like that." I paused. "Unless you're ready for this to end?"

She didn't speak for almost a minute. "Does anyone ever say no to you, Dylan?"

It wasn't typical in business.

Not in my personal life either.

From a young age, I'd learned how to get what I wanted.

Still, I needed to make something extremely clear, so I said, "Alix, I've told you, you can always say no to me."

She leaned her face into my hand. "I told you, I don't think I can."

I remembered the last time she had said that to me.

I lifted my head and pressed my lips against the shell of her ear, whispering, "I'm never going to let you go."

The color her cheeks had turned told me she liked my response.

What I didn't tell her was, in that moment, I knew this girl was going to be my wife. And, at some point soon, I would make that happen.

There had been so many women in the past.

None mattered.

None measured up.

They had all been steps that led me here.

Alix was the one.

It wasn't her vulnerability or the way her lips touched my skin when she nuzzled my hand or how her eyes revealed everything to me—all things I liked very much.

It was her smile.

That slight lift of her lips told me everything would always be okay.

And it would be.

As long as I had her.

FIFTEEN

ALIX

PRESENT DAY

I ARRIVED a few minutes late to the restaurant.

I was nervous about having dinner with Smith, but that wasn't the reason I was here twelve minutes past eight.

That was because it had taken me a while to get out of bed. To get myself together. To put on enough concealer to cover the darkness under my eyes and the puffiness around my lids.

At one point during my life, I'd barely worn any makeup.

That wasn't true anymore.

I loosened the light scarf from my neck and unbuttoned my jacket as I walked into the restaurant. "Hi," I said to the hostess as I reached the desk she was standing at. "Reservations for Smith Reid."

She glanced at her tablet. "Yes, I see it right here. Looks like the other member of your party has already arrived." She looked up. "Please follow me."

I stayed behind her as she led me into the main dining room.

I wasn't more than a few steps in when I saw Smith.

He was sitting at a table against the window on the other side of the room, and he was typing something into his phone.

As though he could sense my arrival, he gazed up.

Our eyes locked.

I could feel his stare.

It hit my face first.

My chest.

My legs.

It wasn't a feeling I was used to.

Not unless it came from Dylan.

My God.

As I closed the gap between us, still quite a distance away, I compared Smith to the pictures I'd looked at of him online and the small details I remembered from the night we'd met. He was photogenic. There wasn't a bad shot of him. But he was definitely more handsome in person.

That made me even more nervous.

He stood when I was only a few feet away, the hostess already gone, leaving us completely alone.

"Alix, thank you for coming."

There was two seconds of awkwardness. He didn't know whether to shake my hand or reach in for a hug.

I solved the problem by lifting my fingers into the air.

When he gripped them softly, I said, "Sorry I'm late."

"Not a problem."

I pulled my hand away and moved to the other side of the table, hanging my jacket and purse over the back of the chair. My nerves were making me unsteady, so I was careful when I sat down and pulled myself closer to the table.

It was a moment.

Eventually, once I calmed down, I'd be able to celebrate it.

"How's Joe doing?" I asked.

He placed a napkin on his lap and gazed back up at me.

His expression was suddenly full of worry, the same amount he'd worn when the medics put Joe in the ambulance.

"The doctor isn't happy with the way his kidneys are functioning, so he's trying a new course of treatment. I'm sure he'll be discharged once his numbers level out."

The worry faded, and in its place was a look I recognized.

He was exhausted.

"Have you been spending a lot of time at the hospital?" I asked.

"His ex won't go, and she won't let their kids see him. The rest of his family is in California, and he doesn't want them to know."

"That leaves you."

He nodded.

He was a Rose.

A tingling flared in my stomach, causing me to shift in my seat.

"He's at the best hospital in Boston," I said. Since I'd read the paramedics' notes, I knew which one they had taken him to. "I have all the faith in the world he'll have a full recovery."

I smiled at the way his eyes lit up.

I couldn't help it.

"Thank you again for what you did." The grin was still there; it had just turned a little more serious. "You handled the situation so well. I'm assuming you must work in the medical field."

My job wasn't listed on my profile online. Neither were my hobbies.

There was just an emoji under my name.

A sun.

"I'm a dispatcher for the Boston Police."

He pointed his face a little to the side, as though he was going to emphasize what he was about to say. "Well then, I'm impressed with the city's training. For not being out in the field, you knew exactly what to do and what to look for, and your diagnosis was accurate. You'd make an excellent paramedic and an even better doctor."

"The thought of going to med school isn't exciting."

"Neither is law school."

"But you made it, and now, you're an attorney. So, how did you survive?"

His personal profile didn't have anything about his work on it, so now, he knew I'd looked him up.

He didn't seem affected by it.

Maybe he was just hiding his reaction.

He was an attorney.

He knew how to do that as well as I knew CPR.

"Every time I wanted to quit," he said, "I would think back to the way my father had treated my mother and then how he'd fucked her. That was all the motivation I needed."

It took two sentences for me to learn that Smith hadn't had an easy childhood.

And that he was a Massachusetts native because a little bit of an accent had popped out.

As I opened my mouth to respond, a waitress came to our table and asked if we wanted anything to drink.

I waited for Smith to tell me what his recommendation was for dinner and the red wine that would pair well with it.

But it wasn't Smith who did that.

It was Dylan.

Will I ever get used to this?

"Champagne, please," I said.

The waitress then looked at Smith, and he voiced, "Tito's and soda with two limes."

Not even their drink orders were similar.

If Dylan wasn't having wine, he preferred his booze straight with no ice.

"I'm sorry," I said to Smith after the waitress told us the

specials and left. I wanted to get this out before he changed conversations. "I didn't know your decision to go into law was such a personal one. Had I known, I never would have gone there."

"No need to apologize. I could have given you the answer I say to everyone else, but I decided to get personal."

As he stared at me, I wasn't sure how to respond.

Part of me wanted to hide beneath the scarf because this amount of attention was overwhelming. The other part of me wanted to ask him why he had chosen to tell me about his family.

"What made you get into dispatching?" he asked, saving me from making that choice.

Dispatching was a job, not a career. It wasn't something anyone dreamed of becoming. You went in and worked your shift and the rest of the ones you were scheduled for that week.

Month after month.

It was the same.

"All my life, I wanted to work in the medical field. While I was finishing my undergrad, I realized med school wasn't for me. So, I stayed in Boston and started working for the city."

"I'm going to take a guess and say, Boston University." Before I could reply, he continued, "No, I'm going to retract that and go with Northeastern."

There were over thirty colleges in Boston.

"How did you know?" I asked.

He laughed. "Wait a minute. I'm right? You really went to Northeastern?"

The look on his face told me it had truly been a guess.

I was relieved to hear that he hadn't looked me up.

"Yes," I said. "You're right."

As he laughed, he gripped the edge of the table with both hands, and his head tilted back.

It was the most laid-back sound.

I wondered if I'd ever laugh that way again.

"My sister, Star, goes there," he told me. "I know the campus well."

"She's getting her master's?"

He shook his head. "Bachelor's."

She was much younger than him.

From my estimate, at least by ten years, which put Smith somewhere in his early thirties.

The same age as Dylan.

"So, you went to school in the Back Bay, and you work in the city. What do you do for fun, Alix?"

I met my best friend for happy hour several times a week.

I spent time with Dylan whenever he came home.

I dreamed about waking up to a sunny day.

"You're going to laugh," I said.

This was a question I was comfortable with.

He put his elbows on the table. "I won't."

"I'm from Maine. This small, quiet, quaint town in the southern part of the state. While I was living there, I craved noise. I used to play the radio just so I could fall asleep at night."

"You wanted a city."

"More than anything. When I was seven, my parents brought me to see the Boston Pops; my dad had won tickets through work. My dad parked along Mass Ave., and the second I got out of the car, I knew this was where I'd live."

"Why would I laugh at that?" His voice softened.

Dylan's never did. He was all business, all the time.

That was something they didn't have in common.

And it surprised me enough from Smith that I looked up at him, realizing that, at some point, I had broken contact to stare at my empty plate.

"Well, you asked me what I did for fun. My answer is Boston."

He continued to gaze at me for several seconds before he said, "I want to view the city through your eyes."

"What do you mean?"

"Show me what a day in the life of Alix is like."

I squeezed my napkin with every bit of strength I had, and then I twirled it around my fingers. "It's not that interesting, I assure you."

"I've lived here almost my whole life. I left for college and law school but came back right after I graduated. I don't think I appreciate the city the way I should. I want you to change that for me."

"That's a lot of pressure."

He smiled, and it was warm.

Heat I could feel all over my skin.

Skin Dylan had touched just this morning.

"I think you're more than capable," he said.

He was asking me out again without using any of those words.

As I attempted to respond, the waitress returned to our table.

She set the cocktails down and took our dinner orders.

And then, once again, we were alone.

Smith held his vodka and soda into the air and said, "To Joe."

"To Joe."

When his glass clicked against mine, our fingers brushed.

It was just enough contact that I had to go searching for my breath.

SIXTEEN

ALIX

PRESENT DAY

WITH MY HEAD on the pillow, I faced Dylan's side of the bed, waiting for the familiar noises.

The slight squeak of him opening the bedroom door.

The sound of him walking on the floor.

I heard none of that.

The room was silent, except for the quiet murmur of HGTV.

Dylan was punishing me for going out with Smith tonight.

I should have expected this.

I shook my head, angry that the fluffy down was so soft, wishing it were hard, that it would hurt me, that it would take away everything I was feeling.

I'd left the restaurant this evening with Smith's phone number saved and a date at the end of this week when we'd be spending the entire day together.

When I got home, I climbed into bed and hoped Dylan would show up.

That he'd put his hand on my lower back.

The same place Smith had put his when he walked me outside after dinner.

Something was wrong with all of this.

I didn't know how to fix it.

I didn't know if I could.

I just knew I was completely in love with Dylan Cole, and Smith Reid had made me smile tonight.

I gripped the blanket with one hand and the pillow with the other. I opened my mouth, and everything I was feeling came out.

This time, it was a scream.

One that the entire row of townhouses could hear.

SEVENTEEN

DYLAN

THREE YEARS AGO

WE WERE a month into our relationship, and I had started to learn everything about Alix Rayne.

It was a period that had gone by quickly because I took it in as fast as I could, and I stored it, so I wouldn't forget.

When it came to her, everything was important.

It was the smallest details that made the biggest impact.

Like the afternoon I'd brought fries to the firehouse from the pushcart in Quincy Market. Fifteen large bowls for everyone on duty to share.

Not my baby though. She got her own. One I'd drizzled with vinegar and salt with a side of ranch and ketchup. She liked to alternate dips.

She was so taken aback by the gesture, especially when she saw I had brought her both condiments.

But I wanted to do more than just feed her addiction to fries.

I wanted to be able to look at a menu and know what she would order. I wanted to pair that meal with a wine she would enjoy. I wanted to know what sentiments made her smile, what movies caused her to cry, why her skin always smelled like lemons.

I had gotten those answers within the first thirty days.

During that time, the only nights we'd spent apart was when she was on for her twenty-four-hour shift, which she did twice a week.

If we weren't at our jobs, we were together.

And then things began to move fast.

There was no reason to slow them down.

She wanted to go to sleep next to me, and I wanted to wake up next to her.

There was only one small bit of turbulence.

Alix hated to fly.

And the size of the five-seater, single engine that I used for personal travel made her anxious as hell.

It took a few weeks of talking to her about it, showing her the aircraft and where she'd be sitting, before she even started to warm up to the idea.

Eventually, we went.

I kept the first trip short. Twenty minutes. Just enough for her to get comfortable with the space, to feel the different shifts of wind and how they moved the plane, to get used to the view while she sat next to me in the cockpit.

It was a lot to take in for someone who didn't like to be in the air.

During the next flight, I extended our airtime to forty-five minutes. I got her to laugh after takeoff and hold my thigh instead of gripping the seat while we descended.

I continued to work on her, gradually increasing our flight time, landing at different airports around New England where we'd go to lunch before I flew us back to Boston.

Bar Harbor, Maine, was our first overnight trip.

Alix had always told me her heart belonged to Boston. It was true; she fucking loved that city. But she had a connection to Maine that was just as strong.

I really got a chance to see it during that vacation.

After our first night there, she woke me up at a little past three in the morning, and we hiked to the summit of Cadillac Mountain. Depending on the time of year, it was one of the first places in the US to see the sun rise.

Alix wanted to share that with me.

When we got to the top, we sat on a slab of rock several feet from one of the ledges. We'd arrived early enough to see the dawn break and the black start to lift from the sky. There were mountains surrounding us in the distance with Frenchman Bay right below. Several small islands dotted the dark water.

It was a gorgeous sight.

Especially when the ball of red began to lift, turning the sky a burnt orange and a bleeding pink.

I glanced to my left where Alix was sitting. Her eyes were on the sun, and the warmest fucking smile was spreading over her face.

I knew in that moment why I was here.

It was to see that expression.

The look she gave when she stared at something she loved.

"It's so beautiful," she whispered, still facing the sunrise.

"It is." My answer had nothing to do with the sky.

Hell, I wasn't even sure I remembered I was still on top of a mountain.

I was gazing at her, feeling things, thinking of a future I hadn't ever considered before.

What made Alix Rayne so different than all the other women I'd dated in the past?

Many things.

The biggest was the way I'd felt when I stood next to her at the table the night I met her and every moment I'd spent with her since.

Happiness.

That was what filled me.

From the way she looked at me, spoke to me, listened to me, and reacted to my touch—they all made me feel it.

"Dylan?"

I shook my head, running my hand over my morning scruff. My stare rose from her lips to her eyes, and I saw she was finally looking at me. "Yeah?"

"One day, I want to spend my summers here. Get out of the mugginess of the city, rent a small cabin somewhere down there"—she pointed at the islands below—"and come up here every morning to watch the sunrise."

I pulled her across the rock until she was sitting between my legs, her back leaning against my chest. "I can't believe you're telling me that I'm going to have to wake up *every* morning before four and haul my ass up here."

She laughed.

Goddamn it, that sound was pretty.

"We don't have to hike it *every* time." She chuckled again. "Once in a while, I'll let you drive us to the top."

I wrapped my arms across her, my hands resting over her navel, and we watched the sun move higher in the sky. It'd changed colors from the last time I looked at it. Now, a light pink and a deep navy were reflecting off the clouds.

There wasn't even a ripple in the bay.

Just stillness all around us.

I pressed my mouth to the top of her head, inhaling the scent of her hair, breathing it in several times. "I'm going to make it happen."

"What?"

"You're going to be spending your summers here." She turned to look at me, and I added, "I promise."

We could do it now.

I could certainly afford it and work remotely for those few months.

But Alix wouldn't leave her job, and I'd never ask her to.

Her brows lifted as she tried to read me. "You'd move to Maine for me?"

"I would."

Her expression changed.

It warmed.

And then I saw that look again—the one she'd had when she was watching the sunrise.

"Kiss me," I told her.

She climbed higher on my chest, slowly reaching my mouth. Her hand went to my cheek, and she pulled me as close as she could get me.

Her eyes told me she loved me.

So did her kiss.

EIGHTEEN

ALIX

PRESENT DAY

I RUSHED inside the police headquarters and into the call center. Just as I was passing Marla's door on the way to my workstation, I heard, "Hey, Alix."

I turned around, backing up, and stopped in her doorway. "Are you looking for me?"

She pointed to a bouquet of flowers on the corner of her desk. "Those came for you this morning."

I stared at the arrangement, trying to think of who would have sent them.

I didn't like any of the conclusions I had come up with.

"Are you sure they're mine?"

I could tell the question surprised her.

With a smile, she said, "Your name is on the card, so I think they're for you."

I thanked her and took the vase, placing it next to my computer. My purse went in the bottom drawer, and I put on the headset.

I didn't open the envelope.

I wasn't ready.

Instead, I sucked in a deep breath and rested my fingers on the keyboard, my thumb gently tapping the space bar but not hard enough to actually press it down. My body tensed. The tips of my toes ground into the bottom of my shoes.

It was time.

I hit the key that would connect the incoming call and said, "Nine-one-one, what's your emergency?"

"I've been in a car accident. I'm on the corner of Huntington Avenue and Cumberland Street. No one is hurt, but both cars are pretty banged up."

My chest loosened.

Air slowly made its way through my lips.

The tapping stopped.

But it would all start up again when I took the next call.

At the end of my shift, I logged out of the system, grabbed my purse and the flowers, and went into the restroom.

I locked the door behind me.

I needed privacy.

Silence.

To get this over with before I left for the night.

What I didn't need was a coworker watching how I reacted to the card.

I slipped my finger under the flap of the envelope and lifted, slowly removing the thick paper inside.

THANKS FOR HAVING DINNER WITH ME LAST NIGHT.
I'M REALLY LOOKING FORWARD TO OUR NEXT DATE AND TO
FALLING IN LOVE WITH BOSTON AGAIN.
—SMITH

I read the note a second time.

A third.

The same thought kept popping into my head.

Smith?

I hadn't expected him to be the sender.

I wasn't disappointed.

I was flattered he would go through all the trouble of finding where the call center was located and sending me something so beautiful.

I held the note against my palm and looked up to see my reflection in the mirror.

The smile on my face was growing.

As I touched my cheek, my skin was becoming so warm; the color flushed.

Affected.

Just in a different way than I'd thought.

I slipped the note inside my purse and brought the flowers downstairs and into the backseat of the car I'd ordered. While the driver moved into traffic, bringing me to the other side of town, I took out my phone and clicked on Smith's name to send him a text.

Me: The flowers are gorgeous. Thank you. That was so nice of you.
Smith: I'm glad you like them.
Me: First dinner, and now, this. I hope you know none of it is necessary, but it's certainly appreciated.
Smith: You saved my best friend's life, Alix.
Me: I only called 911. The paramedics and the staff at the hospital are the ones who saved his life. Please don't feel like you have to repay me or that you owe me anything. All I want is for Joe to be all right, and it sounds like that's a strong possibility.
Smith: The flowers were because I wanted to try to make you

smile, something I enjoyed looking at when I sat across from you. Our next date is because I want to see you again. Once you showed up to the restaurant, it was no longer about Joe. It became all about me.

As I continued to stare at the screen, I could tell my face was turning warm again, my skin reddening.

I typed out a few sentences and immediately deleted them.

I tried again.

I couldn't make anything sound right.

I didn't know how to respond.

But I felt like I needed to say something.

I was sure he'd looked at my pictures online, so I replied with an emoji he'd seen under every one.

A sun.

"It looks like we've arrived," the driver said as he pulled up in front of Rose's building.

I thanked him and went up to the call box outside the entrance, hitting the button next to her name. She buzzed me in, and I made my way up to her place.

"You brought me flowers?" she asked after she opened the door.

"No, someone bought these for me."

I recognized her expression.

It was the same way mine had looked when Marla told me the arrangement was for me.

To alleviate her concern, I said, "Don't worry; it's not from who you think."

I carried the flowers into her kitchen and set them on the counter.

She followed me and stood in front of the bouquet, sticking her nose into the petals to smell them. "There's no card."

I took the heavy paper out of my purse and handed it to her. Then, I moved to the end of the counter to grab the bowl of chips.

"Wow, you're right. It's not at all what I was thinking." She looked up and grinned. "But I like where this is going, and I *looove* that date two is already in the works."

"He asked me before dinner was even over." I shrugged. "It felt right."

"Of course he asked you—because you're fabulous. I'm just not sure why you're defending yourself right now."

I hadn't realized I was doing that.

But I was.

More for me than her.

Because, in my mind, I had to justify why I would go out with Smith when Dylan was still very much in my life.

Since I didn't know what to say, I lifted the bowl of chips and carried it out of the kitchen. On my way to the living room, I passed a table that was covered in framed photos.

One caught my attention.

The same one I saw every time I came here.

I never commented on it.

Never gave it too much attention.

But that had been before my date with Smith.

Before I felt the guilt that was eating at me right now.

Rose stopped at my side and said, "It might be time to update some of these pictures."

"But that's such a good one of all of us."

Dylan and I were on the left side of the photo, standing on top of Cadillac Mountain. Our arms were in the air, and we were flexing our muscles.

Before the hike, we had agreed to haul ass up the mountain since Rose and Terry were joining, and we'd refused to let them beat us.

They hadn't.

We'd won by several minutes.

On the other side of the picture were Rose and Terry with sad, defeated, sweaty faces.

"That whole trip was amazing," she said.

I was quiet while I thought about that weekend—the incredible food and wine Dylan had arranged for us, the evenings we had spent talking until it was almost time to wake up for our hike.

The laughter.

"It was perfect," I agreed. I shoved in another mouthful of chips and swallowed. "God, he's so handsome."

"Best eyes I've ever seen."

I looked at her. "You're so right about that."

"I remember when he locked eyes with me at the restaurant the night we first met him. There I was, trying to be all badass, stopping him from touching you. He gave me this stare as he handed me his wallet, and the whole time, I was thinking to myself, *There's nooo way Alix is going to be able to resist that man*."

"I gave in quickly, didn't I?"

She laughed. "You did, you ho."

I smiled, shaking my head.

She rested her chin on my shoulder and said nothing for several seconds. "I know it's hard, having that chapter of your life over."

It wasn't over.

I just couldn't tell her that.

So, I leaned my head against hers, leaving it there for a moment, and then I stepped to the side and gave her the chips. "Take these before I eat them all."

"You'd better not be full. I have the usual on its way over."

That meant a pepperoni and mushroom pie from the Italian

place on the next block and two slices of chocolate cake from Nona's Bakery.

"You know I can always eat," I told her.

That was a lie.

Because, tonight, I wasn't feeling very hungry.

NINETEEN

ALIX

PRESENT DAY

THE CREAK of my bedroom door opening woke me out of a dead sleep.

With my eyes closed, my heart pounded inside my chest. My fingers clenched the blanket and pillow, squeezing them into my palms.

"You came." I took a breath. "I didn't expect you. I thought ..." There was a knot in my throat. It felt larger than the width of my tongue. It hurt when I swallowed, when I tried to inhale, when my lips pressed together to say, "I thought you weren't going to come home again since I told you I was having dinner with another man ..."

I waited for him to tell me we needed a break, that this was the last time he would be coming back here.

Seconds ticked by.

It felt like thousands of them.

And then I heard, "I love you."

A whimper came out of my lips, and I slapped my hand over my mouth, trying to hold back the noise.

"I love you so much, Alix."

Oh God.

Tears began to fall.

Fast.

Dripping over my hand and onto the blanket.

My nostrils flared as I sucked air in through my nose and released it just as quickly.

My muscles quivered.

My body tightened as I bent myself into a ball. "Dylan ..." I sobbed, no longer able to keep it in. "I'm so s-sorry. I ..."

Fucked up?

Should have stayed home?

Shouldn't have put Smith's flowers on the kitchen table?

I didn't know.

I just knew I was sorry we were in this situation.

Sorry there were tears running down my face.

That I didn't know what to say to him.

That he didn't know what to say to me.

"Dylan, I d-don't know w-what to d-do." I reached for the pillow from his side of the bed and hugged it against my chest. "I'm trying my b-best here."

I hated that this hurt so much.

That my heart felt like it was going to explode.

"Alix ..." I heard his feet move over the floor as he came closer. "Do you want me to stay tonight?"

"Yes."

I didn't even have to think.

The answer to that would always be yes.

There was movement on the bed, and then I felt the warmth when he wrapped around me.

My throat began to loosen.

My hands released what they'd been squeezing.

The tears stopped.
And dried.
I was asleep again within minutes.

TWENTY

DYLAN

TWO YEARS AND ELEVEN MONTHS AGO

THREE MONTHS.

That was how long it had taken me to tell Alix I loved her.

It wasn't that I didn't feel it.

That emotion had been present since almost the very beginning.

But I had known, once those words were spoken, I would need to have things in place.

That started with our living situation.

Alix stayed with me during the nights she wasn't at work. She kept her things at the apartment she shared with the three firefighters and brought over what she needed.

I wanted her to move in with me.

My interior designer was working on a mock-up for my walk-in closet where half the space would be converted to fit Alix's needs. She was also putting together a design for the master bathroom. Alix liked taking baths, so she was about to get a much larger tub and a place to sit and do her hair and the little makeup she wore.

I hadn't told her about the renovations.

Or the details of my business.

Or anything financial-related.

She didn't know my net worth, the extent of my investment portfolio, how this was one of my three homes.

Things like that didn't matter to Alix, so I never brought them up.

She didn't give a shit about designer clothes or five-star restaurants or that the bracelet I had given her several weeks ago cost a year's worth of her rent.

She cared about helping others.

Saving lives.

Being at the right place when someone needed her.

But, if she was going to be my wife, she needed to know everything.

I decided to approach the conversation a little differently.

So, I flew us to Lake Tahoe for a long weekend. Once we landed, we were picked up in a Suburban and driven about fifteen minutes to my home.

She grinned when we pulled into the wooded driveway and turned her body toward me. "What is this place?"

"It's a house."

She bent her head to be able to see the top of it out of the window. "Why would you rent something so big for just the two of us?"

It was just under ten thousand square feet and built into the base of the mountain with a full view of the south side of the lake. It was too big for a family of ten.

"Because I wanted you to see how beautiful it looks from each window."

Her stare slowly shifted back to me. "But it's the size of my old high school."

"It's my place, Alix."

"What?" Her eyes widened. "You really own that?"

I nodded. "I also have a condo in LA where my West Coast office is located."

She glanced from me to the house, repeating that pattern every few seconds. "Does someone usually live here?"

She was processing this in stages.

"No, the homes are available to *us* whenever we want to stay in them." I reached across the seat and put my hand on her cheek. "We're going to look at places in Maine soon."

"I had no idea," she said softly. She glanced around the car as though she just realized she was in it. "I take that back. I knew something based on the way you live in Boston, but I didn't know things were like this."

"Does it bother you?"

Money was the reason most women wanted to date me.

That was how different my relationship was with Alix.

"No," she said honestly. "I just don't know this world at all, and I'm trying to keep up." Her serious expression turned to laughter as she added, "Dylan, I have three roommates; we all share one bathroom, and that feels perfectly normal to me. And, last week, I bought baby body wash because it was cheaper than the adult soap, and that's what I shower with at work. I know nothing about having money."

My hand dropped to her waist, and I pulled her across the seat until she was right next to me. "I know this is a lot to take in; you don't have to do it all at once."

She seemed to think about my comment. "I'm going to work on it, I promise, but we have to come to an agreement on something first."

She was laying out the terms like this was a business transaction.

It was sexy.

"Let me hear it," I said.

"If we do get a place in Maine, I want to pay for at least half."

"Deal."

"And I want it to be small and intimate and cozy, so you're always close to me." She gazed at me through her lashes. "When we're in Maine and away from our jobs, I always want you to be near me."

Fuck me, this girl is special.

Outside this SUV was a six-million-dollar home that had been featured in *Architectural Digest*.

That meant nothing to her.

She wanted a hundred-thousand-dollar shack in Maine where she could see me from every room.

That was what I loved about her.

I put my hands on her cheeks and pulled her face up to mine. "I'm going to tell you everything this weekend; nothing will go unspoken. You will know all about my business and what it has grown into and the investment projects I'm involved in on the side."

"I can assure you, it's not going to change the way I feel about you."

"Good, because, one day soon, that house out there is going to be half yours."

Her breathing changed.

Her pulse quickened as I slipped my hand down her neck.

The tip of my nose brushed hers, and she closed her eyes.

We hadn't even gotten out of the car.

It didn't matter.

"Alix ..." I grazed a thumb over her lips. "You weren't in my life for more than two seconds when I knew I loved you."

Her eyes flickered open.

That look returned to her face.

The one she had worn during the sunrise on top of Cadillac Mountain.

"I love—"

I smashed my lips over hers, not letting her say another thing.

I didn't need to hear it.

I already knew.

And I'd be listening to those words for the rest of my life.

TWENTY-ONE
ALIX
PRESENT DAY

IT WAS A SUNNY DAY.

One where I didn't have to work, so I went to Newbury Street to take some photos.

I was trying to be more active on social media, making an effort to post a few pictures a week.

I had so many followers; I felt pressure to keep them entertained. They came for the sun. That was what I believed anyway, so I needed to give them plenty of it.

Shot after shot.

Today, the object of the photo shoot was my hand as I held a cup of coffee and the way the sun made my skin glow. I zoomed in to the skin between my thumb and pointer finger as it surrounded the cup, the way the diamonds in my bracelet sparkled from it.

I took close to thirty pictures with my phone, and I posted the one that had come out the best.

Normally, I would have gotten up and gone back home.

That was where I was comfortable spending most of my time.

But I didn't have the urge just yet.

What pulsed inside me was a carefree sensation I hadn't felt in a long time.

My life was usually too structured to feel that.

I had too many rituals.

But the sun was making me smile.

It was making me feel good.

And so were the notifications that came across my screen, showing all the emoji replies.

If visitors commented, they weren't allowed to use words. That was the one rule I'd set when I opened this account. It was respected for the most part. When it wasn't, the comment would get deleted.

I took a break from my phone to peek at the people passing the bench. Most were in such a rush. I wondered where they were coming from and where they were headed.

If they appreciated sunny days as much as I did.

If they would recognize me without my hat and sunglasses on.

I let that thought simmer while I glanced down at my cell again, seeing a text from Smith flash across the screen.

> Smith: *We're still on for tomorrow?*
> Me: *Yes.*
> Smith: *I'll pick you up. Just let me know what time and your address.*
> Me: *This is my day of planning, so I'll pick you up.*
> Smith: *I've never had a date start that way before.*
> Me: *Sounds like you've been on some pretty shitty dates.*

That sounded more like Rose than me. I just needed something punchy to prevent him from coming to my townhouse.

It was a home I shared with Dylan.

It didn't feel right, bringing Smith there.

Smith: Ha!
Me: Send me your address. I'll see you at 11.

Hours later, while I was sitting in the living room of my townhouse, I pulled up the photo I had posted earlier and checked who had liked and commented on it.

Rose had left an emoji.

I continued scrolling and saw Smith's name.

My heart started to pound.

He had liked the picture.

He had followed me, too.

I clicked on his profile, my finger hovering over the button to follow him back.

Right before I pressed it, my attention was dragged away when I heard a sound from the kitchen.

I hoped it was Dylan coming home early.

I waited.

One second, two seconds.

Nothing.

Slowly, I glanced back at the screen, my finger still in the same spot.

I wasn't sure why I was even contemplating it.

I hit Follow.

Then, I immediately got up from the couch and went over to the ottoman to get my purse. Once I found my keys inside, I placed them in the bowl on the table in the entryway, and I set my bag on the closest barstool in the kitchen.

I followed the steps.

Each one.

And I waited for Dylan to come home.

TWENTY-TWO

ALIX

PRESENT DAY

WHEN THE CAR pulled up to Smith's townhouse, I climbed out of the backseat and walked up his four front steps. I pressed the doorbell and waited for him to answer.

I was so nervous; my back was covered in sweat.

My hands were shaking.

They trembled even harder when he opened the door.

I couldn't believe how good he looked.

The first two times I'd seen him, he had just come from work and was all dressed up in a suit.

But, now, he had on a pair of Converse with khaki shorts, a polo, and an NYU hat.

Fancy wasn't my first preference.

This was.

And it made him even more handsome.

"Hi." At some point, he'd said the same thing to me; I had just been too busy taking him in to respond. "Are you ready to go?"

He shut the front door behind him. "I'm all yours."

My face flushed.

My hands wrapped around the crossbody strap of my purse just so I had something to grip.

With no idea what to say, I laughed and turned around to head for the car. Once I got into the backseat, I tried to relax.

I wasn't expecting to feel this jittery.

It wasn't the coffee I'd had this morning or the empty stomach I had right now.

It was him.

"I think you should give me a hint," Smith teased as the driver pulled away from the curb.

He sounded so sweet, and it caused me to smile. "You're getting nothing out of me. The whole day is going to be a surprise."

A grin came across his face, and he looked out his window.

"Is that where you went to school?" I asked. "NYU?"

When he glanced at me, a warmth spread over my chest.

"Yeah, for both of my degrees."

"Why'd you pick it?"

"It's one of the top law schools in the country, and it's only four hours from Boston."

"Were you one of those kids who went home to do laundry?"

He sighed, and that was when I heard the pain in his voice. "No, I went home to take care of my mom and sister."

I pushed myself into the corner of the seat, wishing it would just swallow me. "Smith, I'm sorry. This is the second time I've done that to you."

"Don't apologize. The truth is, she never got it together after the divorce. That's why I came back after law school and why I haven't left."

He was getting personal again.

It didn't freak me out.

It actually made me want to know more.

"Where does Mom live?"

He rubbed his hand over his lower thigh and said, "At the moment, a place in Roxbury."

Roxbury was a suburb of Boston that didn't have the best reputation.

It certainly wasn't where I'd want either of my parents living.

"I know what you're thinking," he said, now staring at the hand circling his knee. "But I've tried everything. She doesn't want help, and she won't let me get her out of there because she says she'll have to walk too far to buy drugs."

"Smith ..." I waited for him to look at me. "That's not what I'm thinking at all."

In my line of work, I heard stories like this all the time.

A large percent of our emergencies were drug overdoses.

It was a language I knew extremely well.

"How long has she been using?"

His eyes showed me the answer before he said, "Since I was a kid, years before my dad left. When he took off with everything, she lost it, and her periods of sobriety never lasted more than a few weeks, even when she was pregnant with my sister."

I had been afraid he was going to say that.

"But it sounds like your sister is doing as amazing as you."

"She's the only good thing that came out of my childhood." His eyes lit up when he spoke about her. "Once she graduates and finishes law school, she's coming to work for me."

"What an incredible big brother you are."

He shook his head. "No, she's just a hell of a kid."

Dylan's story was nothing like Smith's.

Both men had different types of pain, experiences, things that had fueled them to become self-made entrepreneurs.

Smith's was just a lot darker.

And it didn't sound like his situation was getting any better.

I turned my head toward the window and saw we had

reached the South End. We drove two more blocks, and then the driver parked along the curb.

"Thank you," I said as I opened the door and climbed out, waiting for Smith on the sidewalk.

His hand went to my lower back as I led us toward the front of the building.

I didn't push his fingers away.

I liked the way they felt.

Right before we reached the entrance of the bakery, I stopped and looked at him. "Most people wouldn't begin the tour here."

"You're not like most, Alix. I learned that the night we met."

I smiled and tried not to let the tone of his voice affect me. "I've become somewhat of a foodie, which means I eat like a pregnant woman."

He laughed. "There's nothing wrong with that."

"Except I have this thing for chocolate cake, and I like to start my mornings with it. I've scoured the entire city to find the best. And it's here"—I pointed at the door in front of us—"at Nona's. So, this is what we're having for brunch." I paused. "You do like cake, don't you?"

I tried to remember some of the food pictures he'd posted and if any were of dessert.

He laughed again, his grip on me becoming a little tighter. "Of course I do."

I opened the door, and the smell of chocolate hit me in the face.

"Damn," I heard him say from behind me. When I looked over my shoulder, he was gazing at the display of cookie sandwiches that were filled with buttercream frosting. "You've got good taste, Alix."

TWENTY-THREE

DYLAN

TWO YEARS AND NINE MONTHS AGO

FIVE MONTHS.

That was how long Alix had been in my life.

Within that short amount of time, she'd moved in with me. My interior designer had remodeled Alix's side of the closet, and my master bathroom was in the middle of a full renovation.

The changes were for her—to make her feel more at home in my place.

But neither project had kicked off as smoothly as I wanted.

Because, once I showed her the mock-ups my designer had put together, Alix had shot down both ideas. She didn't want a bigger tub, and she certainly didn't want half the closet.

It all came down to money and how she didn't want me to spend any on her.

Spoiling her was one of my favorite things to do, and I had no plans to stop.

That was what I told her whenever she tried to fight me on the construction, and it would shut her right up.

That girl only ever wanted one thing.

My time.

I did a hell of a job giving her plenty of it.

Until I didn't.

That was what led to our first serious argument.

It had taken place over the days leading up to a holiday weekend.

I'd been working eighty hours a week for several weeks straight, only coming home to shower and change before heading back to my office. My business was growing, and with that came more responsibility than I'd ever imagined.

Since I'd been spending so much time away from Alix, I decided to take her to Lake Tahoe for the long weekend.

She'd enjoyed our last trip there.

She'd like this one even more.

I made sure she didn't have to work, and I cleared my schedule. I put in to have maintenance and cleaning done on my private jet for the morning we were supposed to leave.

The last thing I'd expected was for the plane to already be booked.

As I searched our system, I saw that the entire fleet had been reserved for the whole weekend.

I had nothing to fly.

No way to get us to the other side of the country.

Alix suggested we take a commercial flight.

I laughed at the idea.

I was the owner of an extremely well-known, successful private airline. My days of flying commercial had long been over. The last thing I needed was my competition seeing a picture of me stepping onto a Delta flight.

I'd be the butt of every goddamn joke in the industry.

So, I canceled the trip.

Alix and I would hang out at home—something we hadn't done in at least a month.

But, as the weekend approached, I received a call from the

realtor I'd hired in Maine. She'd gotten a tip on a house in Bar Harbor that hadn't yet hit the market. The pocket listing was everything I wanted—two stories directly on the water with unobstructed views, a boat dock, private driveway, four bedrooms, and five bathrooms.

It was perfect for us, and it was an incredible investment opportunity as well.

All I had to do was convince Alix that this was the house we should spend our summers in.

The night I was going to talk to her about it, I got back late, knowing she'd already be home from her shift.

Except she wasn't.

And she didn't walk through the door until after midnight.

I'd been sitting in the dark living room.

Waiting.

For three fucking hours.

My patience thinning as my texts had gone unanswered.

When she finally came in, she went straight to the fridge, grabbed a beer, and drank it without even shutting the door.

As she put down the empty bottle, I said, "Didn't you get my messages?"

She took out another beer and brought it into the living room, sitting in the seat across from mine.

There were bags under her eyes and paleness to her skin.

"I saw them come through," she said. "I just didn't have a chance to get back to you."

She'd had a long day.

I'd had one, too.

But that didn't excuse her from ignoring me.

"I deserved a response, Alix."

She circled the bottle over the armrest. "There are times when I just won't be able to give you one."

I sighed, shaking my head.

That answer wasn't good enough.

Not when I'd been waiting hours to hear from my girlfriend, not knowing if she was dead or alive.

"You work through the night and in some of the worst parts of town. You don't get to choose when you can and can't write back to me. You pick up that goddamn phone, and you let me know you're all right."

"I couldn't." Her voice turned sharper. "I had blood all the way up to here." She pointed at her elbow and then said, "And I didn't want to get it all over my phone."

I'd caused the snappiness in her voice, not the patient.

But I just wanted her to understand what tonight had been like for me.

"I've been texting you for hours, Alix. I can't imagine you were covered in blood that entire time."

She was quiet for several seconds, her thumb sliding up and down the glass. "Dylan, I don't think you have any idea what I do for a living. The lives I'm responsible for. The duties I have to perform on a minute-by-minute basis." Her expression softened. "I can't just pause in the middle of inserting an IV or stop performing CPR to answer my phone. I'm out there to save lives, and that's all I'm trying to do."

I understood that.

And I respected it.

But she was missing the point.

"All I'm asking is for you to be a little sympathetic when it comes to my fears."

"It isn't always about you." She immediately stood and moved into the archway of the room, leaning her shoulder against the molding. "I don't know what you want from me." Her voice was so fucking quiet.

She was hurting.

And I was only making it worse.

I stood and moved over to her, putting my hands on her waist. "You're tired," I said as I pulled her against me. "You had a long shift, and it wasn't an easy one. Why don't you go upstairs and take a hot shower? And we'll talk about this in the morning during our drive to Maine." I kissed the top of her head, breathing in her lemon scent. It came from the ambulance and the chemicals they used to keep it clean and the antibacterial gel she lathered over her hands.

"We're not going to Maine tomorrow."

I squeezed her a little tighter and waited for her to glance up at me. "The realtor found us a house to look at in Bar Harbor, so I booked us a suite at our favorite hotel. We're going to leave in the morning."

"I can't go."

I leaned back, making sure I could read her expression correctly. "Why can't you?"

"I picked up two extra shifts, so I have the next twelve hours off, and then I'll work forty-eight hours straight."

My stare shifted between her eyes, and when I saw she wasn't bullshitting me, I said, "Why the fuck would you do that?"

She wiggled out of my grip and took several steps back. "Why wouldn't I? You canceled our trip, and we had nothing planned. They were offering holiday pay, and I need the money to help go toward the down payment on the house."

I hated when she said that.

All she had to do was ask, and I'd give her anything she wanted.

That included paying off her student loans—something I'd offered to do many times and I was always turned down.

I never complained when she took extra shifts.

But, this time, it was interfering with my plans.

"Tell them you're no longer able to work."

Her hands went to her hips. "I'm not going to do that."

"You don't want to go to Maine?"

"This has nothing to do with Maine, Dylan. This has to do with you respecting my job." She took another step, her back now pressed against the wall. "I'm not you. I can't just call and say I'm not coming in. If I don't show up, they'll be short-staffed, and people can go untreated."

"They'll find someone else to cover it."

"They don't need to."

"Make this about us, Alix."

She turned silent.

And both of us took several deep breaths.

She was the first to break when she said, "I'd like to at least see some pictures of the house."

I ran my hand over the whiskers on my cheek. "That's something I need to talk to you about."

"Why?"

"I upped our budget and added a few additional requirements."

"Was the size one?"

I nodded.

"No, Dylan." Her face dropped, her eyes now focused on the ground.

I'd lost her.

"Hear me out," I said, waiting for her to look at me again. "I want an investment home in Maine, and I can't have that with the budget you've given me. Since we'll only be there during the summer, I want to rent the place for the remainder of the year. With that in mind, the realtor found a house that fulfills what I need."

"You promised."

She sounded hurt.

She didn't need to be.

She was getting Maine, she was getting me away from my

office for several months at a time, and she was getting a house that would be so much nicer than the kind she wanted to buy.

"I did; you're right, but that was before I saw what rentals were going for in Bar Harbor."

One of her hands clung to the molding while the other moved to her chest. "Small, intimate, and cozy, so you're always close to me."

"Quaint isn't going to make me money, Alix."

"For once, that's not what this home is about. It's supposed to be a place we decide on together where I can pay half of the mortgage."

"You can still contribute."

"Contribute? Are you even listening to yourself?"

I laughed at the dig. "Now, you're just trying to ruin the night."

"You're an asshole," she snapped, and she walked to the stairs.

"You're not the only one who had a shitty day."

She stopped halfway up and turned toward me. "Because signing up millionaires to fly with you is so incredibly stressful."

"That's uncalled for."

"You know what's uncalled for? The three deaths I witnessed tonight. Two because my CPR wasn't able to revive them and a third because I couldn't climb ten flights of stairs fast enough, and the elevator wasn't working. Those three faces are what I'll see when I go to bed; the cries from their families are what will keep me up all night." She gripped the banister, emotion suddenly filling her eyes. "I've only ever asked you for two things: more time together and a small house in Maine. And you couldn't even give those to me."

She climbed the rest of the stairs and slammed a door.

Later, after I left my home office, I saw which one it was.

It was the guest room.

I jiggled the handle to open it.

She had locked it.

She wanted me out.

So, that night, we slept in separate beds.

As I climbed into the king-size we usually shared, knowing she was just a few rooms down the hall, something hit me so fucking hard.

Alix and I weren't perfect.

We had cracks.

And, as the months passed, I learned some deepened while others got filled in.

I also learned that wasn't the last night I'd sleep alone.

TWENTY-FOUR

ALIX

PRESENT DAY

MY DATE with Smith had started almost twelve hours ago.

It still wasn't over.

Following the cake we'd had for brunch, we went for coffee by the harbor and rode bikes through the Public Garden. We visited the Public Library and had French fries at my favorite pushcart outside Quincy Market. Then, I finished the evening with a Red Sox game, snagging us seats in the Green Monster.

After the win against the Blue Jays, we grabbed gelato several blocks past the stadium, carrying the small cups to a bench that overlooked the busier part of Lansdowne Street.

I was surprised by how fast today had flown by.

And how I found Smith so easy to talk to.

I hadn't told him anything too personal—I certainly never brought up Dylan—but the things I had said came out so comfortably.

Now, half a day had passed since I picked him up at his town-house, and I wasn't looking for an excuse to go home.

I was enjoying these moments.

All of them.

Even the one we were about to have, which was a conversation I'd been avoiding. When Smith had mentioned his best friend earlier today, I could tell the topic hurt him.

But I still had to know.

And, with it being so late, I was running out of chances to ask him. "How's Joe doing?"

He took the spoon out of his mouth. "It's ugly, the whole situation. After everything I've gone through with my mom, seeing Joe like this is fucking killing me."

"He's using?"

"Minutes after I brought him home." He shook his head as though he was remembering what that had looked like. "He's supposed to go to rehab in a few days. I'm positive he won't."

"Maybe, once he hits rock bottom, he'll change his mind."

"He lost his wife, and he's about to lose his kids."

I'd treated hundreds of addicts.

I knew this disease better than anyone.

"Trust me, Smith; it can get much worse."

He was quiet for several seconds before he said, "You know what hurts the most?"

"That you can't do anything about it?"

He nodded, and the look in his eyes emphasized his answer even more.

"I'm sorry." I held the cup of gelato against my lap. "The helplessness can feel so overwhelming, I know."

There was nothing in my mouth when I started grinding my teeth together.

No gelato, not even the spoon.

I was just rubbing enamel over enamel.

And it had everything to do with the tingling inside my chest.

Vulnerability was the most attractive trait in a man.

I never saw it in Dylan.

And, now, I'd seen it multiple times in Smith.

"What's your best friend like?" he asked.

Rose.

The perfect distraction.

"Honestly, she's like a bull in a china shop." I laughed at the description I'd used. "She's brutally honest and unfiltered and the most loyal person in this world."

"I want to meet her."

I hadn't expected him to say that.

Rose would love the idea.

And she would love him.

The thought of that blew my mind.

Because of Dylan.

Because we had just spent last night together, and now, I was on a date with Smith.

And I'd taken him to the places I frequented most in the city.

Spots that meant something to me.

Like the French fry vendor outside Quincy Market.

And then, tonight, I would hopefully be with Dylan again.

This was fucked.

On so many different levels.

But that didn't stop me from smiling at Smith and saying, "I'm sure I can make that happen."

He glanced past me down the long street, and I watched him take in the people who passed us, slowly spooning in several mouthfuls of gelato.

Then, he turned his head once more, and our eyes locked. "I was hoping you had the ability to change my mind about Boston."

Heat pooled into my face. "Did I?"

"Yes." When he exhaled, I heard the air come through his nose. "I want to see you again, Alix."

I glanced away but still felt his stare on me.

Something inside me was aching.

Breaking.

Screaming.

Because I wanted to see him again, too.

And it was wrong.

So fucking wrong.

But, with Dylan not here to stop me, I gazed back up at him, chewing the inside of my cheek, and said, "I'd really like that."

"When are you free?"

I thought of my schedule and replied, "Two nights from now."

"Dinner?"

I grinned. "Only if we can start with cake."

"I have a better idea." He tossed the gelato container into the trash bin next to our bench and faced his body toward me. "Let's eat at my place. I'll cook."

His place.

An intimate space.

With just the two of us.

"You cook?" I asked.

"I had to feed my sister, so that forced me to learn."

More vulnerability.

More redness seeping into my cheeks.

"I haven't mastered my way around the kitchen," I told him.

"I'll teach you."

I wanted to be Smith's student.

I wanted to watch him do something he enjoyed.

The same way I had watched Dylan fly.

This was another moment.

And I felt the celebration in every part of my body.

"Dinner at your place sounds fun," I finally answered.

His stare intensified.

Sensations began to pound inside of me—more tingles, more bursts, more electricity that shot into every muscle.

I stood and walked to the trash bin several feet away.

I needed space.

I needed air.

I needed to tame these feelings before they became out of control.

The half-eaten gelato was tossed into the bin, and as I turned back toward where he was sitting, I quietly gasped.

He'd left the bench.

He'd followed me.

And, now, he was directly in front of me.

In my space.

Taking all of my air.

"There's something about you, Alix ..."

I was frozen.

I wasn't even sure I was breathing.

"What is it?"

He gazed at me.

He didn't even blink.

"I don't know, but I can't seem to get enough of it."

When I broke contact to look at the ground, he stepped forward, and I felt his hand on my face.

I heard myself gasp again.

It was so quiet.

And so loud inside my head.

I didn't pull his fingers away.

But I lifted my chin.

That was when I heard his exhale again.

He was fighting something.

I knew it had to do with me.

I watched as he pushed through it.

As he moved closer.

As his other hand lifted in the air and landed on the other side of my face.

"Smith ..."

"Don't stop me." His voice was filled with so much passion.

His neck bent toward me.

His mouth was now inches away.

I should wiggle out of his grip.

I should take several steps back.

I should tell him I couldn't do this.

But I didn't.

Because I wanted this.

My eyes closed.

I sucked in some air.

And I felt the warmth of his fingers as he gripped me even harder, pulling me the last bit of distance before there was none between our faces.

It was just skin against skin.

It felt like so much more than that.

The tension in my body left.

My limbs turned numb.

The only thing remaining was the prickling in my chest.

As I breathed past it, I reached forward and put my hands just below his neck.

He felt different than Dylan.

Relief caused my fingers to tighten, and I clenched the polo between them.

My lips parted.

I took in his tongue, circling it with mine.

Dylan's scent was bold and spicy.

Smith's was gentle and enticing.

Both drew me in.

Both held me.

Both made me want more.

It felt so good to inhale Smith's cologne.

And it made me miss Dylan's.

God.

Still gripping his shirt, I used it to pull his body against me.

Our torsos clicked like puzzle pieces.

My arms wrapped around his neck.

It felt perfect.

That was a terrifying thought.

And an exhilarating one.

I felt the power in his hands, the movement of his tongue, and my mind went to a place where they were on my skin.

Our kiss deepened.

And I wondered ...

Can I really have an affair with this man?

I knew that answer immediately.

But the questions didn't end there.

There was one more.

Could I fall in love with him?

As I considered it, Smith's lips slowly left mine.

The warmth from him stayed, and so did the taste of him on my tongue.

His nose rested against my cheek, and the hand that had been there was now circling my waist.

He was fighting something again.

So was I.

"I'm going to order you a ride home," he said, pulling back to look in my eyes. "As much as I want to get in that car, I'm not going to."

Gentle.

Even more enticing.

And, now, I could add patient to that list.

Before I had an opportunity to respond, he added, "This is the second best day I've ever had in Boston."

My palms slid down his neck and stopped at his chest.
The hardness of his muscles made my face turn even hotter.
"What was the first?" I asked.
"The day I moved my sister into her dorm at Northeastern."
I knew then ...
Without any doubt ...
I was in so much trouble.

TWENTY-FIVE

ALIX

PRESENT DAY

Rose: I'm up for work, staring at my phone, wondering why there's no text from you. Unless you're still with him? In that case, you're forgiven. But, if that isn't the case and your ass went home alone and you didn't text me, you're in serious trouble, lady.

THE REASON she hadn't heard from me was because Dylan had come home last night. And he had gotten my full attention seconds after I climbed into bed.

I turned over to face his side of the mattress and saw he hadn't stayed.

I deserved that.

I was surprised he had even shown up after I spent so much time with Smith.

But he had.

And he'd made love to me.

And, now, I was by myself again.

I tucked the blanket over my head, so I wouldn't have to look at his unmarked pillow.

Me: Sleeping. Go away.
Rose: At least give me an emoji, so I know how things went.

I added a sun.
But then I deleted it.
In its place, I put a blushing face with puckered, kissing lips.

Rose: Shut the fuck up. I need details, woman. I'm calling you right now.
Me: Let me wake up first and get some coffee in me, and then I'll give you a call in a little while.
Rose: At least tell me where it took place.
Me: It happened after the game in the middle of Lansdowne Street.
Rose: You spent the WHOLE day with him? What went down after the kiss?
Me: We got in separate cars, and I went home.
Rose: Are you going to see him again?
Me: Yes, on my next day off.
Me: I'm pretty certain you're going to love him.
Rose: You really think this guy can handle me?
Me: I think he's going to surprise the hell out of you.
Rose: Because that's what he did to you yesterday, isn't it?
Me: He's nothing like him, Rose.
Rose: Do you want to talk about it?
Me: No.
Rose: You know ... yesterday was such a beautiful, sunny day.
Me: That made it even more perfect.

TWENTY-SIX

ALIX

PRESENT DAY

I WOKE TO A SOUND.

It was one I didn't hear that often.

One that made my entire body tense.

That halted my movements and made me still inside my bed.

There was a chance I'd only hear it once.

That the skies would clear, and the noises from the storm would quiet.

While I waited, I stabbed my nails into the blanket, clinging to the material as though it were holding me. As though it could pull me out of this world and put me in a place where there wasn't any thunder.

But then it happened again.

The sound.

The cracking.

The unmistakable boom that echoed throughout my bedroom.

I shook like I was swimming in the icy water of Lake Tahoe.

Lake Tahoe.

God, I wished my mind hadn't gone there.

But, as the thunder slapped the air around me for the third time, I knew this was just the beginning.

Of my thoughts.

Of the trembling.

I folded myself into a ball, my arms wrapping over the top of my head.

I was bracing myself.

Because I knew it was about to happen again.

Any second.

I hadn't checked the weather, and I hadn't watched the news, so I hadn't known it was supposed to rain today, that I wouldn't wake up to another sunny day.

The noise went off again.

A *craaack* that was like leather whipping bare skin.

A headache gnawed at my skull.

My stomach churned.

I found it hard to breathe.

This was what happened every time.

Same symptoms.

Same emotions.

Same tremors rocking my entire body.

With each quiver, it felt like the covers were strangling me even tighter.

I had to get out.

I scanned the different spots around my room, looking for a place to run to.

There was the chair on one side. The entrance to the bathroom and the door to the closet on the other.

My feet padded over the floor.

They moved so fast.

And I lunged inside the large walk-in closet.

There weren't any windows.

I didn't turn on the light.

I wanted the darkness.

I wanted the room to feel like it was hugging me.

I was only a few steps in when I fell to my knees.

I didn't shout when the hardness pounded my joints.

When every part of me cried from the impact.

Instead, I crawled.

Each inch of flooring I pulled myself across caused my lungs to restrict even more, caused an ache to shoot all the way up my throat.

I paused.

I dry-heaved.

I did it again.

Nothing but the sound of retching came out.

My stomach finally settled enough for me to keep moving, and I reached the side of the closet.

Dylan's side.

And I wrapped my arms around his suit pants and held them against my chest.

"Help me," I whispered.

Dylan couldn't hear me.

He'd left this morning.

Maybe to fly out before the storm.

Craaack.

My ass hit the floor while my back slammed against the wall.

His pants hung in front of me.

They hid me.

They taunted me.

Craaack.

I gripped every pair that would fit in my hands, and I pulled.

The metal bar they were dangling from broke.

Hangers flew.

Pants dropped all around me.

Bold and spicy.

That was all I could smell.

I wrapped the clothes over me.

I shut my eyes.

I ground my teeth until my jaw felt like it was going to shatter.

Craaack.

I wished it would stop.

I wished there were only sunny days.

Goddamn it, why does it have to rain?

Suddenly, I heard another noise.

This one had come from the bedroom.

It was my phone.

And it was Rose's ringtone.

She was checking on me.

She did that whenever there was a storm.

But I couldn't get up.

I couldn't leave the closet.

I couldn't answer it.

Craaack.

I held the pants against my ears.

My body swayed forward and back, hitting the wall each time.

My mouth opened.

And the scream that came out was as loud as the thunder.

TWENTY-SEVEN

SMITH

PRESENT DAY

I STOOD AT THE SINK, holding my hands under the running water while I looked out the window. The streetlamps showed how hard the rain was coming down, and the few people walking by were all hidden beneath umbrellas.

It was fucking nasty out there.

That was probably the reason Alix was already ten minutes late for dinner.

I'd been looking forward to this evening since the last one we spent together, so I hoped she didn't take too much longer to arrive.

I dried my fingers on a towel and went over to the range, stirring the tomato sauce and flipping the chicken and shrimp I had sautéing in separate pans.

Alix had eaten both during the times we went out; therefore, I knew they were safe to prepare. I'd never forget the way her lips had looked when she opened them to take a bite. How she'd licked the corner of her mouth after she swallowed. Or how, when I'd made her smile, it'd reached all the way to her eyes.

God, she was beautiful.

In a way that made my whole body ache.

An ache that I was having a hard time controlling.

So, I focused on the food, turning down the flame under each burner to prevent it from burning. I was going to add the protein to some fresh pappardelle, mix in the homemade sauce, and serve a rosemary-garlic bread on the side.

But, first, we'd start with cake.

I knew how hard that would make Alix grin, and I couldn't fucking wait to see it.

There was a bakery only a few blocks from where I had grown up that was my favorite. When we were kids, it was where I used to take my sister on her birthday. I'd get her a slice of any flavor she wanted since I couldn't afford a whole cake. This afternoon, I'd made a special trip to that part of town to pick up some for Alix.

I just hadn't known what else to grab for her.

When you were raised like I had been, you learned really quickly why you shouldn't take food for granted. That was why I took pictures from restaurants all over the world.

That wasn't what Alix did.

I'd checked out her profile again this morning, hoping to get an idea of some of the other things she ate and drank, to learn a little more about her.

The pictures of the sun told me nothing.

The little I knew came from the dates we'd been on.

Dates I hadn't wanted to end.

There were so many things about this girl that were different.

I had known that when I received her message, asking if Joe was all right.

She was sweet with a heavy dose of shyness. Mysterious and compassionate. The most gorgeous woman I'd ever kissed.

But what made her so unlike the others were her eyes.

129

They were older than the twenty-something years she'd been alive.

They'd seen moments that were unforgettable.

So had mine.

I could tell nothing could shock her anymore.

We had that in common, too.

The women I'd been with thought they could handle a guy like me.

That was until I woke them during one of my nightmares.

Until they learned how dark my life had been.

I would never allow them to see either, so I would end things after the first few days.

That wasn't the case with Alix.

Instead, I was pulling her in.

Because, when I looked into those stunning eyes, I saw someone who would understand me.

Someone who had experienced pain.

Who still felt it.

And that scared me right down to my fucking core.

I shook my head, taking a drink from the Tito's and soda I'd poured a few minutes ago, and checked the temperature of the champagne. That was what Alix had ordered both times we were together, so I knew she liked it.

The bread was done toasting, and I took it out of the oven.

The chicken and shrimp were ready to be combined.

There was nothing left to do.

Except wait for her.

And, now, she was fifteen minutes late.

I waited another ten before I texted her.

Me: Are you all right?

I shoved my phone into my pocket and carried my drink

into the living room. Once I sat on the couch, I grabbed my tablet off the coffee table and went through a few of my emails. When I looked at the time again, she was forty-two minutes late.

Where the hell are you, Alix?

And why haven't you called me?

Before I had a chance to get back to my inbox, my phone began to ring.

"About fucking time," I growled, the worry dropping from my chest.

That was, until I saw the goddamn screen.

"Mom," I said, holding the phone up to my ear. "What's going on?"

I always took her calls.

Regardless of the time or situation I was in.

And even if I didn't want to deal with her shit.

Like now.

"I need money."

I laughed even though not a word she'd said was funny.

My jaw tightened as my teeth clenched together. "What do you need it for?"

I didn't know why I'd asked. The answer would only piss me off.

"Some motherfucker came into my apartment and took my stash. Jimmy will front me a balloon, but that means I'll owe him, and you never want to be indebted to your dealer, son."

"Jesus Christ."

She never hid it from me.

One of the first things I remembered playing with were caps from her syringes.

I rubbed one of my temples. "How much do you need?"

"Three hundred."

Tonight wasn't supposed to be about this.

It was supposed to be about Alix and getting to know her more.

Goddamn it.

I pressed a button on the tablet and logged into my bank. I transferred three hundred from my account to hers. A confirmation popped up that the money had been sent.

I was enabling her.

I fucking knew that.

I just didn't know how to stop.

"It's there," I told her.

I heard the flick of a lighter. "Could you bring me a carton of cigarettes tomorrow? You know the ones I like. Menthol one hundreds."

I ran my hand over my trimmed beard, fingers digging into my fucking skin. "I just gave you three hundred dollars. You can find your way to a store."

I hung up and poured myself another drink, sipping it while I looked out the kitchen window.

I didn't move.

And, the next time I saw the screen of my phone, it showed Alix was an hour and a half late.

I found her number in my Contacts and listened to the four rings before her voice mail picked up. I didn't leave a message. I didn't put the food in the fridge either. I just turned off the stove and all the lights and made my way upstairs.

Before I got to my room, I sent Alix a final text.

Me: I hope you're safe.

TWENTY-EIGHT
ALIX
PRESENT DAY

IT WAS A CIRCLE.

A never-ending merry-go-round that didn't stop or throw me off.

It just got more vicious after each rotation.

More painful.

It made me wonder when the ride was going to end.

Because it would.

It had to.

I told myself that over and over.

But, during those moments in the closet, the only thing I believed was how helpless I was.

I couldn't escape.

Leave.

Get up.

I was paralyzed.

My ass cemented to the floor, my back glued to the wall.

I was covered in Dylan's suit pants.

Craaack after *craaack* filled my ears.

During the slashes of thunder, I was immediately hit with a memory. The same one. Just a flash of it flickering across my eyes.

In those few seconds, I saw every detail.

Over and over.

And, between each *craaack*, during the periods where there was silence, I tried to remember what normal was.

What it felt like.

How it was a place without pain.

Without memories.

That was only filled with sunny days.

My eyes would close, and I'd think of something that made me smile.

Sitting on a bench in the Public Garden.

Standing on top of Cadillac Mountain.

It wasn't just a picture.

It was as though I were there, experiencing it again.

I could smell the salty air from the summit, feel the crispness of it on my skin. I could hear the wind as it whipped past my face.

I wanted to go.

I would.

But not just to those two places.

I wanted to go everywhere.

So, I would start making a mental list of the places I would visit when I got out of the closet.

Things I would eat.

Tasks I would accomplish.

Then, the ride would turn forty-five degrees.

This was where I felt the loneliness.

It would come out of nowhere.

It would slap me.

Hard.

Directly across the face.

No one could understand how ugly that part got.

Not Rose.

Especially not Dylan.

It wouldn't matter if they were in here with me.

If their arms were wrapped around me. If I heard them tell me I wasn't alone.

It would still eat at me and break me down.

It would leave me with an emptiness, an isolation that could never be filled.

This was what I would have to live with.

Forever.

And then, suddenly, without warning, the ride would turn once more.

Craaack would fill my ears.

And I'd be back in the memory phase.

This would go on for hours.

It held me captive.

Turning, turning, turning until the ride finally came to a stop.

It was the sound of the doorbell that had caused it to halt.

For my eyes to burst open.

It chimed again.

And again.

I felt the chains loosen from around my wrists. The cement cracked beneath me, my back unsticking from the wall, releasing me enough that I could push myself up.

I got onto my knees.

My nails dug into the wood.

I was on my feet.

The ringing continued, not slowing a bit.

Now, it was all I could hear.

Carpet squished between my toes as I moved through the bedroom.

The coldness from the window burned my face as I pressed my nose against the glass.

I looked down at the sidewalk below.

It wasn't raining anymore.

And that made me listen.

And I heard Rose say, "Alix, open the door," between slamming her finger on the bell.

My Rose.

She was here.

She was the reason for all the ringing.

And for all the beeping, I assumed, which was coming from my cell that was somewhere in here, indicating I had a voice mail.

I unlatched the window, lifting it before I said, "I'll be right down."

I went back into the closet to change my clothes.

The ones I was wearing felt extremely wet.

And they smelled of pee.

I didn't remember when that had happened.

I didn't want to.

I threw on a sweater and clean yoga pants along with a pair of running shoes, and I hurried downstairs.

When I reached the kitchen, I slung my purse over my shoulder, and in the entryway, I took the keys out of the bowl. As I opened the front door, I squeezed my body into the small space Rose wasn't standing in, and then I shut it behind me.

Rose's eyes wandered over me as though she were checking for wounds. "I've been ringing the doorbell for ten minutes." She went down to the third step, so we weren't standing so close.

"I didn't hear it."

The worry in her expression grew. "Alix, I've been calling you for the last twelve hours."

"I didn't hear my phone either."

I glanced over her head at the street.

There were puddles everywhere.

But the sky was silent.

That was what mattered.

My gaze returned to her, and I could tell she was on the verge of tears.

"What have you been doing?"

"I was in the closet."

She reached for my hand and led me to the end of the step. "Oh God." Now that I was closer, her arms wrapped around me, and she pulled me against her. "That's what I've been worried about," she admitted. "Every time I got your voice mail, I saw you in that goddamn closet, and the knot in my stomach twisted a little tighter. I really wish you'd just give me a key already."

I squeezed back, knowing a key to my house wasn't something I'd ever give her. "I'm okay."

"I almost called the police."

"I would have killed you."

"I know." She sighed. "That was the only thing stopping me. I was going to give you another five minutes, and then I was hitting nine, one, one."

"Please don't ever do that to me, Rose."

There would be a record of the call.

A thorough description of everything that happened at my house—the things discussed, anything that was witnessed.

There would be questions.

Suggestions.

I didn't need that kind of attention.

Rose pulled away to look into my eyes. "Then, your ass had better answer my call next time." Her hands clutched my shoulders, and her entire demeanor softened. She knew what happened to me during storms, so she knew answering my phone wasn't even an option. Rose just wanted to protect me, and this was her way of trying to do that. "This one scared me, Alix."

"It wasn't any worse than the others."

"It just lasted much longer."

I hadn't known that.

Time didn't exist in the closet.

Her fingers found mine, and she climbed to my stair. "Let's go inside and eat some ice cream. I know you have some."

I stiffened. "I don't have any," I lied, breaking her grasp to move to the sidewalk. "But I am feeling a nice, long walk."

"You want to go for one now? After everything you just went through?"

She was surprised.

She had every reason to be.

Because the last thing I wanted to do right now was leave the only place I felt comfortable.

So, I had to lie again and say, "You've got me craving ice cream." I couldn't even imagine putting anything in my mouth. "A giant sundae," I added. "With extra hot fudge and a handful of cherries."

"You're making me want to drool."

I smiled.

Relieved.

And I stuck out my hand for her to grab.

When her fingers clung to mine, I helped her down the rest of the steps and walked us over to the sidewalk.

We said nothing.

And then Rose broke the silence when we reached the end of the block. "What did you tell Smith?"

I turned toward her, putting my back to the Stop sign. "What do you mean?"

"You were supposed to go to Smith's house for dinner tonight, so what excuse did you give him?"

Dinner.

Tonight.

Smith.

Fuck.

"You didn't cancel with him, did you?"

"It started thundering and ..." I was sure my expression said everything that I didn't. I stared at the ground, wondering what he was thinking and what I would say to him. And then I slowly glanced up. "He was cooking for me."

"You have to fix this."

"I know," I whispered, but I was almost positive no sound had come out at all.

TWENTY-NINE

DYLAN

TWO YEARS AND THREE MONTHS AGO

ALIX HAD REFUSED to call into work, so we didn't go to Maine over the long weekend.

Because she'd been off for twelve hours, which was how long she spent in the guest room, and then she'd worked for two days straight, I had gone almost three days without hearing her voice.

But we texted nonstop.

And I could tell she was trying to respond to my messages as fast as she could.

She'd explained how having a cabin in Bar Harbor had been her dream since she was a kid.

I understood that.

A mansion in Lake Tahoe had been mine.

I'd gotten what I wanted.

There was no reason she shouldn't either.

So, while she was working, I drove to Maine to view the pocket listing my realtor had contacted me about. The house was perfect, and I bought it.

Before I left Bar Harbor, I hired a property manager to turn it into a vacation rental once I had it fully furnished.

Over the last several months, the returns had been twenty percent higher than I had projected.

I was right.

It was one hell of an investment.

But that was all it would ever be because, once Alix got home from her shift, I called the realtor again and told her all about Alix's dream. The following weekend, we flew up and looked at the listings she'd sent us.

Alix fell in love with the third house we saw.

It was a thousand square feet with two bedrooms and a single bathroom.

It didn't have a dishwasher.

It wasn't my taste at all.

But, as we stood on the back deck that overlooked the woods and a sliver of mountain—a view that wasn't even comparable to the house I'd purchased—I could see how much she wanted this home.

She was gazing at me like I was the sunrise on top of Cadillac Mountain.

I turned to the realtor, who was just inside in the kitchen, and I told her we'd pay ten percent under asking price with a thirty-day close.

It was our best and final offer.

I made that clear.

Our offer was accepted two hours later.

Once we were handed the keys, we immediately started going there. With Alix not being able to take any significant time off, our travel extended well past the summer. Neither of us could get enough of that place, and we began flying up every other weekend, never staying longer than four nights.

We ate out every night we were there, dining at the highly rated restaurants around town. The days were spent outside. Sometimes, that meant just sitting on the porch for hours. Other days, we'd kayak or hike. When the snow came, we'd drive to Hermon to go skiing.

Within a few trips, we began to meet some of the locals. We exchanged numbers, and suddenly, we were getting invited to dinners and day hikes. We were even asked to go boating to Nova Scotia for a long weekend.

Maine was an escape.

A comfortable one.

But, soon, we were as busy there as we were in the city.

The biggest difference was neither of us worked much when we were away. I'd check emails a few times a day, return an important call.

Nothing more.

I didn't even have a computer there.

When we were up north, Alix had all of me.

And I had her.

One of the best times we spent there was during the first snowfall. Alix took the week off, giving us a few extra days to stay in the cabin. We skied during the first couple afternoons. On the third morning, we got up late, and Alix cooked breakfast. After we ate, we brought our coffees out on the porch.

It was cold as hell.

I grabbed a blanket and wrapped it around her, putting her sideways across my lap as I sat on one of the chairs. She leaned into my chest, the top of her head tucked underneath my chin.

It didn't matter how hard the sun was shining; the air was far too brisk for the warmth to reach us.

Alix shivered beneath the blanket, and I squeezed her tighter, turning on the gas heater that was above the chair.

She ran her hand over my abs, sighing into my chest, and said, "I never thought I'd say this, but I wish there weren't so much snow."

"You don't want to ski anymore?" I kissed the top of her head.

Alix was a hell of a skier, needing no direction whatsoever.

"No, I do. I love it. I'm just going to really miss our hikes."

I leaned my head back to look at her face. "Who says we can't hike in the snow?"

"We can; it's just more dangerous, especially if there's black ice hiding beneath."

I wrapped a hand around her chin, turning it so that she looked at me. "I've yet to see anything hold you back. Don't tell me the snow is going to be the first thing."

"What if I said it was going to be the cold?"

I laughed. "Then, I'd know you were lying."

Alix would have to be on the verge of hypothermia before she let me bring her inside. It didn't matter how badly she was shivering; this girl loved the cold.

"Does that mean we're climbing Cadillac tomorrow?" she asked.

My smile hadn't faded. "Something tells me you knew where this conversation was headed, and this was your plan all along." My lips disappeared into the side of her neck, two-day scruff rubbing over her skin. "You know it's torture, getting up that early when I'm on vacation."

She was ticklish and couldn't keep quiet or still. "Dylan," she said through laughter, "okay, okay, I'll admit it; it was my plan all along."

"You hustled me." I pulled my face away, my lips now hovering inches in front of hers.

That goddamn look.

The one that was on her face.

The one I could never say no to.

"I'll make a deal with you," she said. "If we check the weather and it's supposed to snow tomorrow, we'll head to the mountain. If it's supposed to be sunny, we'll go for a hike."

I already knew the weather. I'd checked it this morning after I went through my email.

"Deal." I lifted her a little, so I could reach into my pocket and grab my phone. Once I had it, I held it in front of us and clicked on the Weather app.

"I was wishing for a sunny day," I told her as she stared at the picture of the sun that was below tomorrow's date.

Her gaze met mine. "Is that so?"

I nodded.

"I assumed you wanted to go skiing."

"I do." I slipped the phone back into my pocket and wrapped my arm around her. "But I can't bet against a sunny day."

"Why? Is that something special?"

I reached inside the blanket, my hand landing on the outside of her leg, slowly dragging it toward her inner thigh. "Before every flight, my copilot and I have to study the weather that we'll be passing through. We learn to fly through everything. We train for it. But we always hope for sunny days. Those are the easiest, the safest, the ones with the least amount of concerns."

"So, you never gamble against the sun?"

I shook my head, my fingers moving higher until I could feel the warmth of her pussy. "A smart man never bets against something beautiful."

"That would be any sunny day."

I kissed the side of her neck, my lips lowering until they reached her collarbone. "And you."

She moaned, "Dylan ..." as my hand slid underneath the waist of her yoga pants and cupped her pussy, my thumb brushing over her clit.

When her head tilted back, I kissed up her throat until my mouth was on hers. There, I gently bit her lower lip, releasing it to fill the space with my tongue. Once I did, I lifted her, twisting her fully around to straddle me. With the heater cranked up, it was warm enough to slide my sweatpants down my legs. Her pants came off next until there was nothing separating us.

I held her directly over my tip, the wetness from her pussy teasing my crown.

The blanket was gone.

She lifted her shirt from over her head and dropped it on the wooden deck.

Nothing was covering her perfect body.

And not a fucking soul could see it since trees were the only things surrounding us.

She lifted my hands off her hips and put them on the armrests of the chair. Her palms pressed against my chest as she positioned herself.

She was taking what she wanted.

I fucking loved when she did that.

When I could watch her grind over my cock.

Her hands left me, and she lowered until I was fully buried inside her.

"Fuck," I moaned.

Her hips flexed.

Her pussy tightened.

I was going to watch her come.

And then it was going to be my turn.

This was better than any sunny day.

THIRTY

ALIX

PRESENT DAY

MY EYELIDS FLICKED OPEN.

My attention immediately went to the windows across from the bed.

I saw light sneaking in through the closed blinds.

It was a sunny day.

Thank God.

I glanced to my right.

Dylan's pillow wasn't dented.

The comforter didn't even have a wrinkle in it.

He hadn't come home.

When he didn't show up last night after my walk with Rose, I was hoping I'd wake up to him. That I'd feel him before my eyes opened.

I hadn't been that lucky.

At least it was sunny.

That was what mattered most right now.

I pushed myself out of bed and grabbed one of Dylan's shirts off the corner of the chair. I slipped my arms through it, buttoned the middle three buttons, and went over to one of the windows, moving the slats a few inches to get a better look outside.

This was the same window I'd opened last night to speak to Rose.

A memory of me throwing up ice cream flashed in my brain. It'd happened right after I put Rose in a taxi about a block from my place. At least I'd kept it down while she was with me. My stomach just couldn't handle any food after everything that had happened in the closet.

I hadn't even been able to make it home before I puked in the side of a bush.

Like I was back in college.

Except there wasn't a drop of alcohol in my body.

The sickness I'd felt was called life.

Now that I'd gotten some sleep, I felt even worse about what I'd done to Smith. I didn't know how, but I had to make things right between us.

I walked over to my nightstand and got my phone, pulling up the last message I'd sent to him. I immediately started typing.

Me: I'm so terribly sorry about dinner. I feel awful for standing you up. Please let me make it up to you.

My finger hovered over Send.

I wanted so badly to press it.

But I couldn't.

Texting was far too impersonal.

And it couldn't deliver the kind of message I needed it to.

Especially after the texts he'd sent, the last one coming in well past the time I was supposed to show up at his house.

I found his name in my Contacts and listened to it ring once before he picked up.

"Hi," I said, not giving him a chance to speak. "I'm so sorry."

"Are you all right, Alix?"

The tone of his voice reminded me of the night in the alley.

"Yes, I'm fine. I ..." I hadn't planned what I was going to say. I had no speech. No excuses. So, I decided to just be honest. "I had a really horrible day yesterday. I wasn't feeling very well, and I didn't pay attention to the time. I should have called you, and I apologize that I didn't."

He didn't even ask why I hadn't shown up, so I knew I didn't have to give him a reason. But he deserved some sort of explanation even if it wasn't detailed at all.

"I was worried about you."

Rose had said the same thing to me.

Now, I was hearing it from Smith.

My heart clenched.

My stomach did, too, and I wrapped an arm around it to try to ease the tension.

"I'm sorry," I said. I didn't want him—or anyone—to feel that way about me. Not now. God, especially not now. "It was so shitty of me, so, so shitty."

"But you're good now?"

"Yes." I pressed a button on the tablet to open the blinds all the way. I took another look through them, eyes squinting from the sun, and said, "I'm fine. I promise." When he didn't respond, I added, "You need to know I'm not usually the disappearing type."

"It didn't feel like your style."

My fingers were now on Dylan's shirt, fidgeting with the buttons, popping one back and forth through the hole. "I want to see you."

I'd said my thought out loud.

It hadn't even sounded like me—not the tone or the words that came out.

But it was exactly how I felt.

It was what I'd been thinking of nonstop since he kissed me.

When he didn't say anything, I sat on the edge of the bed, rubbing my hand over my thigh. "I fucked up, Smith, and I want to make this right. Let's have dinner together. It'll be on me this time."

"You're going to cook?"

He knew it was a weakness.

That was why I'd wanted him to teach me.

But that wasn't the reason my heart was speeding up, sweat immediately soaking my palms. That was because I'd practically invited him to my townhouse.

I needed to fix that.

Fast.

So, I said, "I'm going to come to your place, and I'll bring something yummy."

He laughed. "I have a feeling you order some mean takeout."

"I do."

"Then, takeout sounds perfect, Alix."

I could tell he was smiling.

I just wished I could see it.

I shook my head as I really thought about what that meant. "How's tonight?" I asked. "Are you free?"

"I'm not, but I can do tomorrow."

I clicked on my Calendar app to check my work schedule. "I'm on for the late shift, so tomorrow won't work. How about Friday?"

That was four nights from now.

Much longer than I wanted to wait.

And that was an admission that terrified me.

"I can make Friday happen."

I stood from the bed. "I'll be over at seven."

He said good-bye and hung up, and I walked over to the

entrance of the closet and took a glance at the racks. They were filled with clothes Dylan had purchased for me.

Before dating him, I'd never given a shit about clothes.

But, once he'd started buying them for me and I saw the way he reacted when I wore them, I'd sought that type of response every day. It'd become my motivation to look nice.

These clothes were for Dylan.

I couldn't wear a single thing in here.

I looked at the screen of my phone and clicked on Rose's name to type her a text.

Me: We need to go shopping.
Rose: For?
Me: My second date with Smith.
Rose: Sounds like someone forgave you. Yesss. How much time do we have?
Me: Until Friday night.
Rose: Girl, that's like a year away.
Me: This is going to be harder than you think. It can't be too sexy. It has to be subtle sexy and mostly casual since I'm bringing dinner to his place.
Rose: I've got this; don't worry. You worry about getting yourself a waxing appointment and making sure everything is bare by Friday.
Me: You're insane.
Rose: No, I'm just determined to get my bestie laid.
Me: God, why does that make me so nervous?

My phone began to ring, the screen showing it was Rose calling. I answered and said, "Are your fingers getting tired of typing?"

"No, I just needed to hear your voice."

"Why?"

"Because you're nervous. About a man. And that hasn't happened in a long time."

She was right.

Dylan was the last man to make me feel that way.

But Rose wasn't going to bring that up, not when this conversation was about Smith.

"It's a strange feeling," I confessed.

"That's because you like him. Obviously."

"I don't know what I like right now. I just know I want to see him again."

"As your best friend, I'm qualified to answer that for you, and I'm telling you, you like him. I can hear it in your voice. And I saw it during our walk last night when I brought up his name."

I briefly closed my eyes, leaning into the entryway of my closet. "He's so different, Rose."

"I know. I mean, I don't, but I do. You wouldn't be talking to him if he wasn't amazing."

I didn't know him well enough to call him that.

But what I had seen so far certainly qualified.

"Will you please tell me I'm right, so I can gloat a little?"

In the time I'd spent with Smith, I'd learned he was patient. Understanding. He was a caregiver, like me; he'd slept in Joe's hospital room so that he wouldn't have to be by himself.

But admitting I had feelings for him was a giant step.

One I wasn't sure I was ready to take.

"You're being ridiculous," I told her.

"Really? Because I'm listening to you being all silent over there; I know you're dissecting every thought and every word, and your head is going in seven million different directions. Why not just make it easy and be honest with yourself?"

I laughed.

I couldn't help myself.

It was almost scary how well she knew me.

"Okay," I finally said, "I like him."

"It's about fucking time. Now, before my head gets too big, I'm going back to work. Please stop stressing. It's not like you're going to sprout a third nipple because you've admitted you care about him."

"You're something else."

"I love you, and I'm hanging up now."

I dropped the phone from my ear and continued to look inside my closet.

I'll need more than just an outfit for our date.

I'll need several in case I see him again after Friday.

Because I want to see more of him.

Because I like him.

Those thoughts were shaking me so hard.

My head dropped toward my chest, and my hands caught my attention.

I was holding them in front of me.

Squeezing them around the phone.

The large, round diamond was shining under the light.

The platinum band was leaving a dent on the side of my pinkie and middle fingers.

I'd put it back on when I was walking home after I threw up.

Rose couldn't see it.

She wouldn't understand.

So, I didn't wear it when I was around her.

Or while I was at work because I didn't want the questions.

And, now, whenever I spent time with Smith since that would just make things impossibly messy.

I'd just have to remember to take it off.

THIRTY-ONE

ALIX

PRESENT DAY

I GOT up from my workstation and went into the kitchen to grab the dinner I'd brought from home.

I wasn't good with the stove or oven, but no one made a sandwich better than me.

Since the police headquarters was extremely busy at all hours of the night, I went outside to an area only employees had access to.

I didn't want to be around people.

I just needed a break from the call center.

I needed air.

This had been the most stressful shift I'd had as a dispatcher.

The phones hadn't stopped for a second, and every call was an emergency. Wait times were double what they normally were. We'd even had to bring in extra police and five sets of paramedics, and they were barely denting the overflow.

My break was supposed to be three hours ago.

Even now, knowing how badly they needed me inside, I was hurrying through each bite.

Halfway through my ham and cheese, I took out my phone

and tapped the screen, scrolling through the notifications I'd missed.

Many were from the picture I'd posted this morning.

I'd taken it outside of Rose's office where I went to bring her some coffee. The sun had hit the mirrored exterior of the building in a way that had to be captured.

I continued to scroll, seeing a few texts from Rose, telling me she found outfits at a boutique near her apartment that she wanted me to try on tomorrow.

There was also an email from the realtor in Maine.

ALIX,
I PROMISED I WOULD KEEP YOU INFORMED, EVEN WHEN I DON'T HAVE ANYTHING TO REPORT. UNFORTUNATELY, THAT'S BEEN THE CASE FOR THE LAST FEW WEEKS. SINCE WE'RE HEADING INTO OUR BUSY SEASON, I SUSPECT TRAFFIC WILL START TO PICK UP. THE HOUSE IS PRICED RIGHT, IT SHOWS WELL, AND INVENTORY IS LOW, SO I ANTICIPATE AN OFFER SOON.
AS ALWAYS, IF YOU HAVE ANY QUESTIONS, DON'T HESITATE TO REACH OUT.
HOPEFULLY, I'LL BE IN TOUCH SOON.
—ANNE

I deleted the email, not wanting to look at it a second longer than I needed to.

That house in Bar Harbor had been my dream home, depleting every dollar I'd saved. Most went toward the down payment; the rest was spread across the monthly mortgage payments.

Dylan could have his fancy place in Boston and LA and Lake Tahoe.

But, in Maine, I wanted basic.

Cozy.

I wanted the home to reflect the one I had grown up in—a place that didn't have frills, but a space where I always felt safe and comfortable, where there was an abundance of love.

For a while, the house did that.

It became our treat.

A rescue from our jobs.

The motivation that had kept us going because we knew Maine would always be waiting for us when we needed it.

But, now, it hurt every time I thought of it.

So much so that I couldn't even go.

I wanted nothing to do with that house anymore.

And I barely wanted anything to do with Maine.

My stomach tightened into a knot, and I put down my sandwich.

Needing a distraction, I swiped my thumb over the screen and came across an earlier message that I'd missed during my first pass.

It was from Smith.

It was a picture of Boston Harbor, the setting sun reflecting off the water. Underneath the photo, he'd written: *There's some shit happening in the city tonight. My news alerts have been going off nonstop. Figured work must be pretty rough for you right now, so I'm hoping this makes it a little better. It's tonight's sunset. It made me think of you.*

My eyes shifted between his note and the photo.

I couldn't believe what I was seeing.

He'd sent me a sunny day.

This man.

As my thumbs began typing on the screen, tears gently sprang to my eyes.

> Me: *You have no idea how badly I needed that.*
> Smith: *I hope it made you smile.*

155

> *Me: It did. So hard.*
> *Smith: Has it been an ugly one?*
> *Me: The worst.*
> *Smith: How are you getting home tonight?*
> *Me: I'm working until the morning, and then I'll probably walk.*
> *I'll need it after this shift.*
> *Smith: Text me, so I know you're safe.*
> *Me: I will.*

I looked up from the screen.

Two police officers had stepped out here to smoke.

It was definitely time to go.

I grabbed my half-eaten sandwich, and as I made my way to the door, I heard, "Hey, Alix."

Up until now, I'd been so careful.

I always kept my head down.

I avoided the more popular areas of the building, using the stairs and back hallways just to prevent this from happening.

I had gone weeks without being discovered outside my department.

And, now ...

This.

I put my hand in the air and waved. "Hey."

"I heard you were back. It's good to see you."

"Thanks." I nodded. "You, too."

The one who had recognized me looked at the other officer and said, "Do you know who she is?"

I couldn't listen to his description of me.

Not today.

So, just as his mouth was opening to answer, I waved again and pushed my way through the door. I rushed up the stairs and hurried to my desk. After I put on the headset, I sucked in a deep breath and rested my fingers on the keyboard, my thumb gently tapping the space bar but not hard enough to actually press it down. My body tensed. The tips of my toes ground into the bottom of my shoes.

I clicked to accept the incoming call.

And I waited.

Me: I'm home.
Smith: You all right?
Me: I'm good, just really tired.
Smith: Try to get some sleep, and I'll see you tomorrow.

My reply was a sun.

It felt much more fitting now.

THIRTY-TWO

SMITH

PRESENT DAY

"I HOPE YOU'RE HUNGRY," Alix said once I opened my front door where she stood on the other side, holding several bags in each hand. "I couldn't help myself, so I grabbed one of everything."

I laughed.

She was so fucking adorable in the baseball hat, her hair in a long braid that hung over her chest. She had on a tank top that tied at her waist and a pair of tight jeans that showed off her perfect legs.

I held out my hands and said, "Let me take them."

She shook her head and stepped inside. "If I give you one, they're all going to fall. Just show me where to set them down."

I brought her into the kitchen, pointing to the large island in the middle.

Once the bags hit the countertop, she faced me. "I'm so sorry again about the other night."

I saw the remorse in her eyes.

"I really wanted to be here," she continued. "I'd been looking forward to it."

I believed her.

And I felt the same way.

I nodded toward the bags. "Show me what you've brought."

"I stopped at four different restaurants." She laughed. "I told you, I eat like a pregnant woman."

"No need to defend yourself. I'm as much of a foodie as you are."

As she took out the to-go cartons, telling me about the dishes she'd ordered, I headed for the cabinets that held the plates. When I got it open, I heard, "Hey, Smith." I glanced over my shoulder at her. "Just grab two forks. It'll be more fun to eat that way."

I liked her style.

I took the utensils out of the drawer and rejoined her, where she'd spread everything out onto the counter. There were French fries, which I was learning was at the top of her food list. There was also a fig and prosciutto flatbread, beef with broccoli, and several rolls of sushi.

Before we dug in, she placed two slices of chocolate cake on the countertop and pushed one toward me.

"You've got to tell me how you started eating dessert first." I sliced off the end bite and popped it into my mouth.

She stared at her fork as she said, "I was at home one night, and I opened the fridge to get something to eat. I wasn't feeling that well, and my options were leftover lo mein or a ham sandwich. Neither sounded appealing, but I knew I had to put some food in me." She looked up, and there was so much fucking pain in her eyes. "There were two slices of cake on the counter, and the thought of chocolate didn't make me want to die. So, I ate one, and the next day, I inhaled the other." She scraped the metal over the icing. "That went on for a long time until it just became normal."

There were so many questions I wanted to ask, starting with her pain, where it had come from, what it was.

I hadn't earned that right.

I was lucky I'd gotten this much.

I swallowed another mouthful and asked, "Is it always chocolate?"

She licked off a large piece of frosting. "Once in a while, I'll grab lemon or red velvet, and I regret it every time."

"You like to switch up the bakeries you get it from because I can tell this isn't from Nona's."

She smiled. "You're getting good."

"You're not the only one who likes cake, Alix."

She crossed an arm over the counter as she leaned into it. "Sounds like you have a bakery I need to try."

"I'll get you a piece next time I'm by it."

I didn't want to mention I'd already done that and make the pain in her eyes look even worse.

"No way. You have to bring me there. I'm so visual; I like to take in the whole experience."

"The place is in Roxbury," I said, referring to the same neighborhood in the city where I'd told her my mom lived. "You won't want to go there."

"But I do."

She had as many questions as I did. I could see them, and I could see her hesitation in asking them.

"Is that where you're from?"

I nodded.

"I'm not new to Roxbury," she said. "I've spent lots of time there over the years. I probably know where the bakery is, and I've probably been on the street where you grew up."

There had been many streets.

We'd never lasted more than a few months in each place.

I took in the last of my cake. "You were there because of work?"

"Yes."

Dispatchers were grounded inside the police headquarters. They certainly weren't cruising the streets of the hood.

"I wasn't always a dispatcher," she said as though she could read my mind.

"What did you do before?"

What they hadn't taught me in law school was how to read people. That was something I'd learned from spending so much time in the industry. That was why, when Alix said, "I was a paramedic," I knew not to ask why she no longer worked as one.

She was extremely uncomfortable.

Every signal was telling me that.

So, I opened the champagne bottle I still had from the other night and poured her a glass. I took a beer for myself and went back to the island.

Her hand gripped the stem, twisting the glass in a circle, watching the fizz float to the top. "Nona's is better," she said, and then she took the last bite of her cake.

"It's still pretty damn good."

Several seconds of silence passed.

She hadn't picked up anything else to eat.

She was just staring at the empty to-go box, running the fork through the frosting that had stuck to the sides of the container. "Hey, Smith?" she said when she finally glanced up.

I was already looking at her.

"Thank you for dropping it," she whispered.

I wasn't sure if she was talking about our last date that hadn't happened or her previous employment. But, when I saw her body slowly start to relax, it no longer mattered.

My mother had once told me, she could always point out a

junkie, even the ones who were trying to hide their disease. She could tell from their pupils, the way they turned to the size of pinpoints.

I could do the same with pain.

One day, Alix would tell me about the demons that haunted her, and I'd know the topics I needed to avoid.

And, one day, she'd know why I never brought anyone to Roxbury.

Holding both mugs, I walked through the kitchen and went out the back door, joining Alix in the garden. This was my favorite area, the space that had sold me on this brownstone. It was so private with greenery on all four sides and not a single building overlooking it.

Alix was sitting on one of the couches in front of the firepit. I took the spot right next to her and handed her the tea I'd made.

She pulled her knees up to her chest and set the mug on top of them.

"Are you cold?" I asked. "I can get you a blanket."

She turned her body toward me. "I'm fine. I actually love the cold."

"So do I."

For all the nights I'd shivered myself to sleep, I should hate it. But the opposite had happened.

"Do you ski?" I asked.

She nodded. "I've seen your snowboarding pictures. Switzerland looked beautiful."

"It was one of the best experiences of my life. It's a place you should definitely check out."

She held the cup against her lips and said, "I'm jealous of all the traveling you've done."

"I didn't really start vacationing until a few years ago when I got the firm to a place where it could operate for a week without me. Now that I have the flexibility, I try to get away as often as I can." I took a drink of the black coffee and set the mug on the table next to me.

"Is it always a different destination, or do you have a favorite that you go back to?" she asked.

I smiled as I thought about some of the sights I'd seen. "I have lots of favorites, but so far, it's been a new spot each time. There are too many things to see to keep going back to the same ones."

"I never used to believe that. Maine was where I wanted to spend my time if I wasn't in the city."

I stretched my arm across the back of the couch, my fingers gently touching her neck. "What caused the change?"

She looked away, and I could tell she was thinking about my question. When our eyes connected again, she said, "I just fell out of love with it."

"That happens. You know my feelings about Boston." I rubbed down her shoulder. "Where do you go when you need a break?"

"I haven't gone anywhere in a while." She was only giving me her profile, but that was all I needed to see how much she was enjoying my touch. She even leaned into my fingers. "But I need to change that."

"What place do you have in mind?"

"Lake Tahoe."

"Incredible spot—in the summer and the winter."

"I was there once, but I never really gave it a chance."

"You should. It's worth it." I reached into my back pocket and took out my phone. "I want to show you something." I flipped through the videos I had saved until I found the one I had been looking for. I then moved closer to her on the couch, holding the screen in front of us so that she could see. "Check this out."

The video had been taken on a ski lift at the top of one of the mountains. The view from two and a half miles up was indescribable. But, from the footage, she could see the lake. In spots, it was teal and then the lightest blue, and in the middle, it was navy. Mountains surrounded the lake. Some were so high; it looked like the clouds were sitting on top of them.

When the clip ended, she glanced at me. "That's Lake Tahoe?"

"You didn't go up Heavenly Mountain when you were there?"

She shook her head. "I didn't see much honestly."

"You have to take the gondola on the south side of the lake up Heavenly. When they let you off, you have to jump on the chairlift, which takes you up even higher. That's where I shot this video."

"That's a sight I have to see." She gazed at the frozen screen and then back at me. "I want to go."

"I'll take you."

I'd get on a plane right now if that meant the pain would just stay out of her eyes.

"You would?" she asked.

Her voice was so fucking soft.

So sweet.

So tender.

I had to touch her.

I placed my phone on the cushion behind me and cupped her face with both of my hands. "I'd really like to."

I'd traveled with strangers before. That was what you had to do when a majority of your friends were married, so going with a girl I'd only known for a couple of weeks wasn't a big deal.

What made it different was that I cared about this girl.

The top of that mountain had changed me.

It would do the same for her.

And I would be there to give her that experience.

To taste it on her skin.

Like I wanted to do right now.

Fuck.

I tightened my grip on her face and pulled her closer until her mouth was inches from mine.

All I could smell was cinnamon.

I didn't know where the scent came from, but I was determined to find out tonight.

I surrounded her bottom lip with my teeth.

It was just a bite.

But it was enough to see how she would respond.

When her body started to loosen and her breathing increased, I knew she was ready for more. So, I closed the gap between us, and my tongue slowly slid through her lips.

"Smith," she moaned.

My hand was now on her navel, and I moved it higher until it rested just below her ribs.

She felt fucking amazing.

I couldn't wait to see her naked.

When I pulled away to kiss just under her jaw, she tilted her head back, giving me all the access I wanted. My tongue grazed her flesh first and then my lips, gradually heading toward her face.

As I hovered in front of her mouth, she reached into my hair and tightly gripped it.

I didn't move.

My eyes just bore through hers.

Waiting.

Until she said, "Kiss me."

It was one of the hottest demands I'd ever heard.

Her fingers released me, and my mouth slammed against hers.

She winced as my thumb grazed her nipple.

Not because I'd hurt her.

That was her way of begging for more.

And that was exactly what I was going to give her.

With my tongue.

Because making Alix feel good was the only thing I wanted right now.

I popped open the button of her jeans. Once I lowered her zipper, I paused, waiting to see if she wanted me to stop.

The only response I got was more moans.

So, I stood from the couch and slipped off her flats. Her pants and thong came off next before I knelt in front of her.

She was watching me.

There wasn't any pain.

Just hunger pouring out of those fucking eyes.

My hands circled her knees and slowly pushed her thighs apart until they were spread enough that I could see her pussy.

Jesus fucking Christ.

It was perfect.

Smooth skin, tight lips, a clit hidden between them that I knew was begging to be licked.

"You're gorgeous," I said, eventually looking at her.

I was so close; each breath I exhaled over her caused her body to bend just slightly.

It was anticipation.

I could feel it.

Because it was pulsing inside me, too, intensifying every second my mouth wasn't on her.

I watched as she stared at me from between her legs.

How she stabbed her teeth into her lip.

How each movement, sound, tug of her fingers on the cushion told me where she wanted me.

And how badly she wanted it.

So, I pressed my nose against the top of her pussy.

My eyes closed, and I inhaled.

Her scent made my cock throb inside my fucking jeans.

More perfection.

I couldn't get enough of this girl.

I started at the bottom, wedging my tongue between her lips, and I gently moved up.

She tasted just as good.

"Oh God," she hissed.

As I glanced at her, her head was falling back, her nails digging into the couch.

When I reached her clit, already so fucking soaked, I flicked it back and forth. It hardened the more I grazed it. Her wetness thickening, her moaning becoming louder. I teased her with the tip of my finger, going in as deep as my nail, opening her just enough to make her crave more.

Her hips bucked, and I licked her harder.

After my tongue circled her several times, I sucked her clit into my mouth, and I drove in a second finger. I twisted my wrist, so she could feel the ridges of my knuckles as they moved in and out of her.

She was tightening around me.

Her hips were moving faster.

"Smith ..." she breathed.

I ground my tongue against her, giving her the friction she needed.

Within a few more licks, she was shuddering, her pussy clenching my fingers. I licked her clit as fast as I could and slowed only when I felt her start to come down.

"Jesus," she panted, her body now still.

I kept my mouth on her, licking the wetness, not pulling away until there was hardly any left.

When I was done, our eyes caught.

I needed her again.

But, this time, in a different way.

"Come here," I said, leaning up just enough to scoop her into my arms. I sat on the couch with her in my lap and held her against my chest.

After a few seconds, her hand went to my stomach, and she ran it up and down my abs. "I owe you ..."

"You just gave me everything I wanted." I pressed my lips into the top of her head and held them there. She wasn't shivering, but I still had to ask, "Do you want a blanket?"

"No."

I moved to the back of her neck, and my fingers slid through her hair. I combed through it several times before I said, "Look at me, Alix."

I needed to know how she was feeling, and her eyes would tell me.

She turned her face to gaze up at me.

The first thing I saw was turmoil.

I'd touched her, I'd gotten her off, I'd seen half of her body naked—it was a lot, all of it.

Maybe more than I had realized.

But what I also saw in her stare was longing.

For me.

And, despite how heavy things looked in those dark eyes, she wanted me.

Still, that didn't stop me from asking, "Are you all right?"

When she nodded, I waited a few seconds, and then I leaned forward and pressed my lips against hers.

The kiss was gentle.

Passionate.

And short.

I pulled my mouth away before I gave her my tongue. "Stay with me tonight."

She was quiet.

She breathed several times.

There was so much confusion in her expression when she answered, "I can't."

She needed time to process.

I wouldn't take that away from her.

"I'll drive you home," I said.

"You don't have to do that. I'll just order a car."

"Alix—"

"Trust me; it's fine," she said. "I just have to grab my phone."

She climbed off my lap and put on the thong and jeans and slid into her flats. Once she was fully dressed, I brought her over to her bag.

She took out her cell and typed something onto the screen. "The driver will be here in one minute."

I waited for her to take my hand, and then I led her through the kitchen and living room until we reached the front entrance. We stood by the door, and I wrapped an arm around her, my fingers resting over her ass.

It felt so good under my hand.

My lips pressed into her forehead. "When am I going to see you again?"

"Soon, I hope."

"When are you off?"

"Two nights from now."

I leaned back to stare at her face. "Then, I'll see you in two nights."

She smiled.

"Is that too soon?" I asked.

"No, definitely not." She glanced through the glass at the same time I did, seeing that a car had pulled up and was double-parked out front. She looked back at me. "He's here."

I needed to taste her one last time.

To have her scent on my lips.
To be closer even if it was only for a few seconds.
"Kiss me."
She did.
And it was everything I wanted.

THIRTY-THREE

ALIX

PRESENT DAY

I GOT out of the backseat of the car I'd hired to take me home from Smith's place and hurried up the five steps to my townhouse.

When I got inside, my keys were placed in a bowl on a table in the entryway, and I set my bag on one of the barstools. I continued walking until I reached the middle of the kitchen.

There were counters on both sides of me.

To my left was wine.

To my right were Smith's flowers in a vase.

They were still alive.

Still beautiful.

Oh God.

I didn't know what to do.

I didn't know how to process what I was feeling.

What made it even worse was when my eyes shifted to the other side of the countertop and saw the note Dylan had written.

And the cup by the sink that he'd left with just a tiny bit of water in it.

And the engagement ring on my finger.

The one I'd put on in the car after I left Smith's house.

Oh God.

My feet weren't steady.

The earth was tilting beneath me, and I couldn't find my balance.

The air I was sucking in was becoming too thick.

The only thing I could feel was the wetness on the inside of my panties.

It had come from Smith's mouth.

This was too much.

Oh God.

My knees hit the tiles.

My body tucked into the tiniest ball.

I gasped in as much air as I could hold.

My mouth opened.

"I'm sorry," I cried as though Dylan were home, pounding my fist on the floor. "I'm so fucking sorry."

I couldn't take the pain.

It was stabbing through my chest.

It was moving to my throat.

It was so powerful; I wanted to gag.

My cheeks were soaked with tears.

My lips were slick with spit.

I was betraying Dylan.

And that killed me.

But I couldn't stop.

And that hurt me even worse.

I liked Smith.

I liked spending time with him.

I liked the way he touched me.

I liked the feeling of his mouth going down on me.

A man besides Dylan had made me come tonight.

And it'd felt incredible.

And it made me feel sick.

I was doing everything I could to keep my dinner down.

Dylan had been the only one for so long.

I'd wanted it that way.

But, now, it wasn't just him anymore.

There was Smith, too.

They'd each get a half of me.

And that would have to be enough.

I rested the side of my face on the tiles, the coldness soothing my sweaty, tear-soaked cheek. I pulled my legs in even tighter, my arms holding them to my chest. "I'm sorry," I whispered.

I wasn't going to make it to my bed.

Not tonight.

Not that it mattered since Dylan wasn't going to come home anyway.

I closed my eyes.

"I didn't mean to hurt you," I said softly.

And then I went silent.

Because I heard the door open.

PART TWO

I remembered the sound of the first beat.
The simple chorus.
The way my hips swayed.
They told me the music would eventually start to play.
They just didn't tell me I would dance again.

THIRTY-FOUR

DYLAN

TWO YEARS AGO

I ASKED Rose to go ring shopping.

I needed guidance.

The only jewelry Alix wore were the diamond earrings I'd gotten her two months ago for our one-year anniversary. Before those, I'd never seen anything in her ears. And, on her left wrist, she always had on her digital watch with a Velcro band. She loved that damn thing. It wasn't my style, so I couldn't even pretend to know what she would want in an engagement ring.

I needed someone to help and to keep me grounded. Someone who wouldn't let me purchase a ring too large that Alix would hate.

That was where Rose came in.

Since I already did so much business with Haifa, one of the best jewelers in Boston, I'd sent him a text earlier this week. He followed up with several questions, and we scheduled a time for me to come in.

On the afternoon of my appointment, I picked up Rose, and my driver dropped us off. We were brought into a private room where Haifa and his assistant were waiting.

Once introductions were made, he pointed at the six ring settings he'd placed on the table. "We'll start with these, so I can get an idea of what she might like."

I lifted the one closest to me, rotating it to the right and left, seeing how the stones ran across the outside and the inside of the band.

The ring was gorgeous, but it would be too much for Alix.

"Each setting can hold up to a six carat center stone," Haifa's assistant told us. "If you're looking for a larger diamond, we can certainly accommodate that—"

"Alix definitely doesn't need a larger diamond," Rose interrupted.

I felt Rose's eyes on me, so I looked at her and said, "She would hate this one."

Her expression told me she agreed.

I set the ring back on the tray and said to Rose, "Why don't you give them some direction, so they know what we're looking for?"

Rose glanced over to Haifa. "Everything on this table is gaudy, flashy, and over-the-top blingy. Alix is simple. She wants to blend in, not stand out."

"Something more traditional perhaps?" his assistant asked.

Rose crossed both arms over the table. "We're talking about a girl who would rather go hiking than go to the spa or sleep in a tent than a five-star hotel. I'm not sure how else to emphasize this, but a six carat isn't her style. Neither is a band dripping in diamonds."

Haifa spoke to his assistant in Hebrew, and then she got up and left the room.

"I have a few ideas," he said. "She's going to pull some different pieces, and she'll return in just a moment."

We sat in silence while we waited.

I wanted to laugh at how accurate Rose's description was.

Alix and I had been together for over a year, and I still hadn't worn off on her. But just because we had varying tastes didn't mean she wasn't supposed to be mine forever.

There was nothing I loved more than her.

Not the business I'd built or the portfolio my fortune was invested in or the air I flew through.

That beautiful woman was going to be my wife.

Whom I would kiss every morning.

Whom I would hold every night.

If that meant I had to buy her the smallest ring in this entire store, I would.

Her happiness was the only thing that mattered to me.

And it was Rose's only priority.

Haifa's assistant quickly returned, placing a tray onto the table. On it were three rings with stones already in them.

"This one," Rose said, lifting the middle one into her hand. She stared at it for several seconds, and then she held it out to me. "You don't have to keep looking. This is the one."

Gripping the ring between two of my fingers, I rotated it around, back and forth. It was traditional in the sense that it was a round solitaire. But it was the details on the band that made this ring even prettier, how it was cut and weaved into a pattern with small etches that streamed off each curve. Every time I moved it, the light reflected off the cuts, and it glowed all around the diamond.

"What do you think, Dylan?"

It was Haifa who had asked, so I looked up at him. "It's beautiful." I then glanced at Rose. "You're absolutely sure this is the one?"

She smiled. It was the first time I'd seen her do that since we walked in here. "I'm positive."

While Haifa described the size of the diamond, the cut, and the clarity—things I'd studied up on over the last few weeks to

179

have a better knowledge of what I was purchasing—I stared at the ring. I pictured it on Alix's finger; I thought of the grin she'd have on her face.

"I'll take it," I said. I reached into my pocket, grabbed my credit card, and set it in front of him. "Charge that for the full amount."

Haifa took the card and said, "I'll get it processed right now."

Once he left the room with his assistant, I turned to Rose. "Thank you."

"Of course. I'd do anything for that girl; you know that." She started to play with her hair. "How are you going to ask her?" When I didn't immediately answer, she said, "You do have a plan, don't you?"

I laughed.

Rose was much more like me than her best friend.

"I'm going to fly us to St. Barts. Rent a house on the beach and propose on the sand. I'll have a chef there to cook for us. We'll have massages poolside. Access to a yacht if we want to go on the water. It'll be total relaxation."

"It sounds incredible."

"I'm kidding, Rose."

She started to laugh, her cheeks turning the same color as her name. "Then, what's your idea?"

"I'm going to take her to Maine. I'll keep it simple, probably a spur-of-the-moment thing because that's what she'll love."

"You're right about that. When do you plan on asking her?"

"Soon." I rubbed my hands over the table, trying to cool down my palms. "I want to get married around this time next year."

"A spring wedding, huh?"

I nodded. "It's a perfect time in the city—not too hot and past the really cold months. After we get married, I'm going to take her on a two-week honeymoon. For the first week, we'll spend half the time in South Africa and the other half at Mount Kilimanjaro. She's going to love it there so much. And then we'll spend the remainder of our time in Europe."

She let go of her hair, her hands now in her lap. She looked at her fingers and then gazed up at me. "You be good to her, Dylan."

"You don't have to worry."

"I always worry. She's my best friend."

THIRTY-FIVE

ALIX

PRESENT DAY

AS I HEARD the creak of the door, my body went completely stiff.

My heart began to pound inside my chest.

My muscles screamed as though I'd hiked Cadillac Mountain twice today.

My body was responding to Dylan as I heard his feet move over the floor.

I hadn't expected him.

Especially not after my date with Smith.

But he was here.

And I didn't know what to do with myself, so I stayed in the ball I was tucked into, keeping my arms over my head and my face pressed into my thighs. "I'm sorry," I whispered when he was right next to me. "I owe you an explanation. I just don't know what to say."

I had to be honest with him.

I certainly couldn't lie.

Not now.

"Do you love him?"

Out of all the things, he had gone straight for the hardest.

When I took a breath, something moved into the back of my throat, jabbing that side of my tongue.

I could barely swallow; it hurt so badly.

I knew exactly what was causing it.

It was the guilt.

Shame.

Disgust.

Because I had to admit to Dylan, "I think I could love him."

There was a spot on my jeans that caught what was running from my nose. Soon, there would be two more circles right above it from my eyes.

"Alix ..."

There was nothing really to say at this point.

He wouldn't tell me to stop seeing Smith or that I was doing something wrong.

"I wanted you to be my future, but someone took that choice away from me."

The more silence that passed, the deeper it dug.

God, this place we were in, it never got any better.

It only stabbed me harder each time and always in a part of my body that wasn't anticipating it.

Day after day.

I fucking hated it.

"I'm sorry," I whispered again.

"Me, too."

My throat tightened as a cry pushed its way out, and I said, "I-I love y-you."

This wasn't a realization.

We knew exactly where things stood.

This wasn't good-bye either.

Saying that would be impossible.

This was us admitting our relationship would never be more than what we had now.

And I truly believed that until I heard, "I wish I knew now what I hadn't known then."

My hand slapped over my mouth, stopping the sob from screaming out through my lips.

Tears were pouring so fast; it felt like my eyes were bleeding.

I didn't want him to leave either.

But voicing that wouldn't change anything.

And removing my hand from my face would just let out the cries I didn't want Dylan to hear.

So, the only thing left to do was to say, "Dylan, I'm not going to make it up to bed tonight."

"Do you want me to stay?"

I felt sick.

I was betraying both of them.

Dylan could smell Smith all over me.

And I was certain, at some point, Smith had known there was someone in my past whom I loved.

The throbbing in the back of my throat was becoming more intense, the longer I avoided the question.

I didn't know why I had delayed giving him an answer.

We both knew what I wanted.

"Yes," I said, "I want you to stay."

Not moving from the ball I was already in, I felt him behind me. I nuzzled in, and a tingling spread to my shoulders and all the way across my back.

It relaxed me.

Calmed me.

It made me close my eyes.

And, just before I fell asleep, I heard, "I love you, too, Alix."

THIRTY-SIX

SMITH

ALIX MET me at my office two nights later. I was in a meeting when she arrived, and once I got out, I found her looking at the pictures on the wall behind my desk. With her back to me, I watched her for a few seconds. Her ass looked fucking incredible in those jeans. Her hair was falling over her bare shoulders, skin I was hoping to kiss tonight.

Before she turned around and caught me staring, I shut the door and said, "Hey, Alix."

She looked over her shoulder and smiled, and then she pointed at the photos. "Are these your favorite places so far?"

That girl.

I just couldn't get enough of her.

I walked over to where she stood and put my hand on her waist, leaning in to press my lips against hers. Tonight, her mouth tasted like cinnamon, and so did her cheek, which I kissed next. "I like having you in here."

"I hope that it's okay. Your assistant said I could wait in your office."

"She's getting fired."

185

She playfully punched my chest.

My hand ran down her side and around her back. When it reached her ass, I kissed just below her ear. "Yes, Alix, those are my favorite places," I said, finally answering her question. I pulled my face out of her neck and looked up at the frames.

"I see Lake Tahoe made the list."

The shot was in the middle of the three rows, taken from the Observation Deck on Heavenly Mountain. "Look at that view. How could it not?"

"I can't wait to see it." As I glanced down at her, she added, "With you."

I wrapped my arm around her shoulders and brought her closer to my chest, kissing the center of her forehead. "What do you feel like doing tonight?"

We'd made plans for her to come to my office but nothing beyond that.

"Isn't there a Sox game on tonight?"

I checked the time. "It starts in about twenty minutes."

"Let's go to a bar and watch it."

She was perfect.

In every goddamn way.

"I'm just going to change out of my suit, and then I'll be ready to go."

I went into the private restroom in the back of my office, placed the suit in a bag for dry cleaning, and put on a pair of jeans and a button-down with a pair of Converse. I slipped my phone and wallet into my back pockets and opened the door.

Alix was sitting at my desk.

"You look good in that chair."

She swiveled to the right and the left and then stood. "It's too fancy for me." She came closer, stopping right in front of me. "I like that the only thing fancy about you is your title."

I laughed. "What does that mean?"

"You're more comfortable in jeans than a suit. Your house could be extremely over the top, but it's tasteful and super comfortable. You want to go to a bar with me and devour a greasy burger instead of chateaubriand."

Someone in her life had to be just the opposite, or she wouldn't have made the comparison.

I didn't care who it was.

"You need to know something, Alix." I put my hands in my pockets, trying to hold back my grin. "I also really like chateaubriand."

"Me, too, but it was the fanciest food I could think of at that moment."

She was so real.

That was another thing I liked about her.

I put my hand on her lower back and led her through the door. "To be honest, I'd probably go for a burger over almost anything." We passed the reception area and stepped into the elevator. "Or pasta."

"I speak fluent pasta."

"I'd like to hear what that sounds like, coming out of your mouth."

Her cheeks flushed at my response, and the elevator door opened. We stepped off and went through the lobby, finally getting outside. I took her just a block away to an old Irish pub that I'd been to many times. We sat at the bar with the TV across from us and both ordered beer and burgers.

The bartender handed us our pints with a basket of peanuts.

"I need to know something," I said once he left us alone. "This is extremely important, Alix."

Her body faced me, and I could see how tense it was. "Okay …"

"Hockey or basketball?"

She relaxed, her face even lighting up when she answered,

"Hockey, of course. I'm from Maine, so that should be a given."

"Good answer."

She took a drink of her beer. "My turn to ask something." Her eyes narrowed, and I watched her think of a question. "Is chocolate your favorite kind of cake?"

I took one of the peanuts, cracked it open, and emptied it into my mouth. "No, strawberry is."

"Really? I didn't know anyone even liked that flavor."

"I do." I ate another nut and washed it down with the spring ale. "So, that means, if you spend more time with me, you're going to have to accept having strawberry in your life."

She laughed, and it was so beautiful—the sound, her expression, the redness that darkened her cheeks.

"What would be your second choice?" she asked.

"Lemon."

"Oh God, that's the one I regret every time I buy it." She was giggling harder. "I don't know if I can finish this date now."

Her body was loosening even more.

Every noise she made sounded lighter.

This was a side I hadn't seen.

And I was going to try my best to keep her right here.

I put my hand on her leg and said, "Whenever you need someone to eat chocolate with you, you can count on me. All I'm asking is, you give strawberry a fair shot."

Before she could respond, the bartender approached and said, "Another round?"

I nodded.

"Please," Alix replied.

I finished the rest of my beer and turned toward her. "I want to know the symbolism behind the sun photos."

She ran her thumb over the glass, condensation dripping onto her skin. When she finally gazed at me, I saw the emotion even though she was trying like hell not to reveal it.

"A pilot once told me, he always hoped for sunny days. They were the easiest and safest and the flights with the least amount of concern."

"In some way or another, that's what we all hope for."

"That's why I share the pictures; we all need a little more hope." She was quiet again. "And some people need the reminder that there will be more sunny days, especially me," she mumbled the last part.

"Why?"

I'd never pushed before.

But this I had to know.

She crossed her legs and put her arms around her stomach at the same time. "I'm petrified of the rain."

I was gentle when I asked, "The rain specifically? Or getting wet?"

She shook her head and didn't respond for several seconds. "The sound of thunder."

I could barely hear her, yet it felt like she was screaming.

I was looking her demon right in the eyes.

Her fear went beyond terror.

I could see it.

Hear it.

A few evenings ago had been one of the worst storms we'd had in a while. It had rained all day and night, the sky shuddering from all the lightning and thunder.

I had a feeling that was the reason she hadn't come over.

That was what had made her feel sick.

She wasn't the only one.

She needed to know that.

I took several sips of the new beer, and then I said, "Do you know what I fear?"

Every night, I had the same dream.

It didn't matter if I only slept an hour or if I got a solid eight; I still had it.

In the dream, I saw a room. The streetlamp shining through the window gave me just enough light to see inside.

I was standing outside the house, my hands holding the frame of the glass.

My sister was in the room, sitting on the floor.

There was no bed. Just a pillow and blanket.

It looked almost identical to some of the rooms we'd shared as kids.

In Star's hand was a needle, and a rubber tourniquet was tied around her bicep.

No matter how fucking hard I banged my fists against that window, I couldn't shatter it.

I couldn't find the front door.

And I couldn't get inside to save her.

I knew what the dream meant.

"Tell me," Alix said. Her voice was still so soft.

"I worry my sister will make a bad decision and turn out just like my mother." Beer wasn't strong enough to hide my demons. I would die with those memories fresh in my head. "I've been trying to protect Star from the minute she was born. I did everything I could, but back then, it wasn't enough." I shook my head. "She's doing so well, and she can lose it all so fast."

She put her hand on top of mine. "We both have our own storms."

Alix wasn't just realizing this. She was just saying it out loud for the first time.

She reached into her purse and took out her phone, pressing something on the screen before she showed it to me. It was a picture of the entrance to Fenway with the sun shining across the lettering.

"You're giving me a sunny day?"

She nodded. "You need it."

She was right.

And she was so fucking sweet.

I leaned toward her and put my hand behind her head, steering her face to mine. When our noses touched, I closed my eyes to inhale her scent.

Cinnamon.

I hadn't realized how much I liked that smell or how much I'd missed it in the last two days.

Or how I couldn't get enough of it.

I closed the distance between us, and her mouth molded against mine, parting only to fit my tongue. My other hand went to her face, and I held her as close as I could get her.

I only pulled away when I needed to take a breath.

Even then, I pecked her lips before I backed up any more.

"Two cheeseburgers, cooked medium, both with Swiss cheese and fries," the bartender said. In my peripheral vision, I saw him place two baskets on the bar. "Can I get you anything else?"

"Cake," she whispered.

I turned to the bartender and said, "Any desserts?"

"I can probably scrounge up some ice cream."

"We're good," I told him.

I knew our food was waiting for us on the counter, but now that I was looking at Alix again, I couldn't glance away.

I needed to know something first.

"Are you going home tonight, or are you going to come to my place?"

She said nothing.

She just looked at me while the emotion came back and played inside her eyes.

Slowly, she seemed to pull herself out of it, and her hands went to my collar, fingers clenching to pull me closer.

I smiled as her lips pressed against my ear.

And, once I heard, "Yours," my dick began to throb.

THIRTY-SEVEN

ALIX

PRESENT DAY

"DO YOU WANT ANYTHING TO DRINK?" Smith asked when we got back to his place.

He walked over to the fridge while I stayed in front of the island, gripping the edge of the counter with both hands.

The buzz that had started to come on at the bar was killed once I ate the greasy cheeseburger and fries.

I didn't want to drink any more.

Tonight, I needed to take in every detail even though this would be one of the hardest things I'd ever done.

Alcohol would make it easier.

It would take the edge off.

It would lighten the guilt that was about to strangle me.

But I'd made the decision to come here, so I needed to be clearheaded the whole time.

"Just some water," I told him.

He grabbed two bottles, unscrewed the caps, and gave me one.

The second I took a sip, I felt his hand on me.

I swallowed.

Barely.

Tingles were bursting all the way down to my feet and shooting straight up to my neck.

The emotions were doing the same. Some were really starting to strengthen, our time together tonight only adding to what I had already been feeling. Some were chipping away at me, like an ice pick breaking up a massive block.

I put the water on the counter.

I tried to focus just on his hand.

It felt incredibly good.

How he reached for the same spot every time, one that was lower than where Dylan's hands always landed.

How his thumb grazed up and down when his other fingers stayed still.

How he used a strength that was much more powerful than I was used to.

I wanted him to feel different.

I wanted them to be nothing alike.

Everything about Smith was hard.

His body.

His past.

His features that made up the most handsome face.

The only exception was the way he treated me, and that was so beautifully soft.

Now that my hand was free, I turned back toward him, and I watched his lips slowly approach.

I wanted them.

I loved the way they felt against mine, how they were so tender.

How, once they touched me, every part of my body would start to respond.

With his tongue on mine, his hands suddenly slid up my sides and stopped right next to my breasts.

His thumbs flicked across my nipples.

They were so sensitive.

I hadn't been prepared for that sensation, so I couldn't stop the moan that came out of me. It was so loud, and it filled the inside of his mouth.

Each time he brushed across my nipples, I made the same sound.

I could feel the wetness in my panties, my clit throbbing to be touched.

My entire body was screaming.

And, as though he heard it, his hand began to lower.

His kisses turned hungrier.

He reached the waist of my jeans and was sliding underneath it.

Having him between my legs was all I could think about.

But that felt like a storm.

The biggest one of my life.

And, because of that, it felt as though droplets were trickling across my forehead. That the wind was picking up, singing caution into my ears.

The sky needed to calm down.

So did I.

Even though this moment was so right, I had to go do something that was so wrong.

I pulled away from Smith's mouth, staying close to his face to catch my breath, and I gripped the top of his hand, so it wouldn't go any further.

I thought of where I could escape to.

It certainly couldn't be his closet.

And then I thought of it.

"I'm just going to use the bathroom," I told him. "I'll be right back."

There was one off the living room, and I walked in and shut

the door behind me. I gripped the sink with both hands, staring at the porcelain bowl, huffing like I'd just climbed ten flights of stairs.

Slowly, I looked up at the mirror.

I was startled by the smile.

This was what Smith had done to me.

He'd created these feelings inside my body.

Along with the ones that were still picking away at my chest.

I was so used to the expression I wore for Dylan; I barely recognized that it was me staring back.

But tonight was different than the last time I had been here.

It wasn't going to end the same.

I was staying until the morning.

And, if Dylan came home, I wouldn't be there.

I just needed … to let him know.

I reached into my back pocket and pulled out my phone, pressing the number for Dylan's cell.

It didn't ring.

It just went straight to his voice mail. "You've reached Dylan Cole. Leave a message."

Beep.

"Hi. It's me," I whispered. "I don't know why I'm even doing this, but it just feels like the right thing." I turned away from the mirror. "Or not … I don't—God, this is so hard." My thoughts were so jumbled; I wasn't making any sense. "I don't know if you planned on coming home tonight." I tucked my other arm around my stomach, hoping the pressure would make it stop aching. "But, if you are, I just wanted you to know that I won't be there." My voice was even softer now. "I'm sorry, Dylan. I'm so fucking sorry. I …"

I couldn't justify what I was doing.

And I wasn't going to.

He knew why I was here.

And he knew why I couldn't make things better between us.

"I hope I see you when I get back home," I told him.

My hand shook as I held the phone to my ear.

I realized what I had just said.

And how badly I had meant it.

"Good night, Dylan."

I ended the call and put the phone back in my pocket.

I turned toward the sink again.

I breathed, shoving the thoughts out of my head as I remembered who was waiting for me in the kitchen.

When the smile returned to my face, I walked out of the bathroom.

THIRTY-EIGHT

SMITH

PRESENT DAY

ALIX STOOD in the entryway of the kitchen, staring at me while I put a bite of strawberry cake into my mouth. I'd taken the slice off the counter, not even the least bit hungry, just to see if I could make her smile.

That was all I wanted right now.

Because, when we had been kissing just a few minutes ago, I'd lost her.

I'd felt it the second it happened, and then she'd pulled away and gone into the bathroom.

But, as I looked at her on the other side of the room, the pain was starting to fall out of her eyes. I could only hope that, by distracting her, getting her mind off whatever was eating at her, I could eliminate it altogether.

So, I held up the plate and said, "Want a bite?"

She said nothing.

I lifted the fork and ate off a chunk of frosting. "I bought chocolate, too, just in case you wouldn't try the strawberry."

I held it out for her to get a better look, and she took a few steps closer.

"It's from the bakery in Roxbury, the one I was telling you about," I said.

I hadn't been sure if she'd come back to my place tonight, but I'd wanted to be prepared in case she did. That was why there was chocolate on the counter and several more slices like it in the freezer.

I watched her stare at the piece.

It had six layers, three of icing and three of cake—all in pink.

Still not giving me a response, I cleaned the rest of the fork with my tongue and dipped it back into the dessert. I took off a decent-sized bite and held it into the air for her. "If you hate it, you can spit it out, and I won't even judge you for it."

The smile was traveling up to her eyes.

Finally.

But she still hadn't moved, so I stuck my tongue on it and said, "Look, I haven't poisoned it."

I saw the fog lift from her eyes.

Her laughter only confirmed it.

I just wondered where she had gone and what would happen if she didn't return to me.

"Open up," I said as I moved the bite toward her.

She surrounded the metal with her lips, and the fork was completely clean when I pulled it out.

There was a lightness to her expression.

It had come fast, and it stayed.

"What do you think?" I asked.

"It's nothing like the fruit." She swallowed. "I expected it to be tart, but it's subtle and really creamy."

"You like it?"

She licked the corner of her lips and said, "It's not chocolate."

Now, it was my turn to laugh. "But it's fucking good, isn't it?"

She tried to hide her smile. "It's definitely better than I thought it was going to be."

That meant she liked it.

I cut off another piece and held it out to her. "Do you want more?"

She nodded and chewed this one much faster. When I was prepping to feed her a third bite, she grinned at me and blinked several times.

That smile.

She was back, and there wasn't even the smallest bit of pain on her face.

I was so fucking relieved.

I set down the fork and put my hands on her cheeks and licked the frosting from her lips. "Strawberry tastes delicious on you."

She laughed again.

God, I'd never get tired of that noise.

I took my time with her mouth, working my hands up and down the sides of her body, taunting myself each time I got close to her breasts.

She was feeling the buildup the same way I was, leaning into me, forcing my hands to splay across her navel.

That was the spot where I wanted to kiss her.

Where I wanted to lick around her belly button before I dipped my face between her legs.

But tonight wasn't about what I wanted.

It was about Alix.

What she needed.

What would make her feel the most comfortable.

My lips fell to her neck and pressed just below her ear, gradually going to her throat and up to her chin. I grabbed her ass and squeezed.

"*Ahhh*," I heard, her fingers running up and down my abs. "Smith ..."

I kissed around the left side of her neck and down to her collarbone. "Do you want me to stop?"

"No," she pleaded. "Please, please don't stop."

With my hands still on her ass, I pushed my cock against her, knowing she could feel how hard I was. And she did because she ground her body against me. I worked my mouth back up until it returned to her lips.

"I want you," I said when I took a breath.

I needed to see her reaction.

To make sure her words matched what I was feeling from her.

Her eyes had turned feral.

Her pulse was hammering away in her neck.

"Then, come have me."

Goddamn it.

I wanted to hear those words on repeat every morning when I woke up.

I didn't wait more than a second before I lowered my hands down her legs. "You're mine now."

I lifted her into the air and carried her up the stairs. When I got to my room, I set her in front of the bed and surrounded her face with my hands.

Before this went any further, I needed her mouth one more time.

I kissed her, feeling her tongue on mine, holding her so tightly against me.

When I let go, I didn't waste any time, instantly reaching for her shirt. I took it off and knelt on the floor to remove her jeans and panties next. While I was down there, I looked up at her. "Jesus," I groaned. "Your body is fucking perfect."

As she processed what I'd said, need pulsed across her face.

The hunger in her eyes increased.

I was sure she was only getting wetter.

With her pussy so close to me, it was easy to check.

I gripped her thighs and steered her toward me, pushing the point of my tongue in between her lips and slowly dragging it up. When I reached the top, I flicked her clit back and forth.

"Smith," she moaned, fisting my hair, rocking her hips forward.

She tasted so good.

I slid two of my fingers inside her, turning my wrist in a circle to grind through her wetness and give her the added friction she needed.

"Oh my God," she breathed.

She was getting louder.

She was constricting around my knuckles.

She was close.

Not wanting her to come yet, I pulled my tongue off her clit, and I stood. I barely had my hands up her body when her lips slammed against mine, kissing me with a hunger I hadn't felt from her before.

She reached for my clothes, undoing the buttons on my shirt and unzipping my jeans. I pulled off the rest, kicking it all to the floor, and then I guided her onto the bed. Once she was spread across it, I went over to the nightstand and grabbed a condom. I ripped off the top and rolled it over my shaft as I climbed on top of her.

When she pulled my face toward hers, she wrapped her legs around my back. Her pussy was aligned with my cock, and I was in up to my crown.

She was pulsing around my dick.

"*Fuuuck*," I hissed at her warmth, at her tightness.

It was a tease.

One I fucking loved.

She nipped at my mouth, her nails digging into my shoulders, heels resting in the middle of my back. "Give me more," she begged.

It was the sexiest command.

I went in a little further, and her moans began to echo in my goddamn ears.

"Alix ..."

She was tighter and hotter, the deeper I went.

"You feel so good."

It took everything I had not to plunge fully inside her, thrusting until the top of her head hit the headboard.

But Alix didn't need to be fucked tonight.

She needed to know how much I cared about her.

And she needed to feel that in every stroke.

I moved in halfway and slid back to my tip, squeezing her nipple while I gave her short, hard pumps. Her head fell into the pillow, and I swallowed her moan as I surrounded her mouth with mine.

She was making every sound I wanted to hear, and she looked so fucking gorgeous while doing it.

I leaned away, so I could see more of her, so I could watch the way her body reacted as I dipped all the way in.

A quick flex of my hips, and I was buried.

She sighed so goddamn loud, spreading her legs even further apart, her mouth now open. "Oh God, yes," she groaned.

My thumb went to her clit, and I rubbed across it. More pleasure was spreading over her face, and her pussy started to close in around me.

"Fuck yes," I growled. "I want you to come."

Her moans got louder.

Her pussy felt even wetter.

I sped up my movements and flicked her clit.

"Smith!" she shouted, her chin tilting up, exposing her whole neck.

From the way her body moved, I could see the orgasm rippling through her. I could hear its intensity from how loud she screamed, how good it felt from the way she was clenching my dick.

When she started to come down, I switched to slow but deep strokes.

That was when her chin dropped, and she gazed at me.

Her hair was a mess. Her lips were ravenous. There was wildness in her eyes.

She'd never looked more beautiful.

I needed her closer.

And I needed her mouth on mine when I came.

I got on my knees and pulled her off the bed. "Wrap your arms around my neck," I told her. Once she did, I put my hands on her ass and pounded back into her pussy. I glanced up at her face just as my balls were beginning to tighten.

"Oh God," she moaned, and I knew she was close again.

"Hold me as tight as you can," I warned before I reared my hips back and plunged inside.

I went in deeper, harder, listening to the sensations she was feeling from the sounds she was making.

Seconds before the orgasm blasted through my balls, my mouth crashed against hers, and I breathed, "Alix ..."

Her pussy clenched.

My movements turned sharper and faster as wave after wave of intense pleasure passed through me. I knew Alix was feeling the same, and I wouldn't let her go. I wanted her as close as possible while I lost myself inside her.

Even after the two of us quieted and stilled, I stayed buried in her pussy.

Her forehead rested against mine.

We said nothing.

We just breathed.

Our hot skin kissing.

Her hands clutching my shoulders.

In this moment, words were meaningless.

So, I tucked my face into her neck, and I hugged her. I was holding her with every part of me, every piece of my flesh that could reach her.

And I didn't let go.

Not even when she fell asleep.

THIRTY-NINE

DYLAN

ONE YEAR AND ELEVEN MONTHS AGO

WE'D ALREADY BEEN in Maine for two nights.

The difference between this trip and the other ones we'd recently taken up here was, I hadn't called any of our local friends to schedule dinners with for when we were in town. For the five days we were here, I didn't want an itinerary. I had enough of that in the city.

I wanted Alix all to myself.

And that was exactly what I'd gotten so far.

We ate, we fucked, and we slept.

It couldn't be more perfect.

But I could tell Alix was getting restless. She wanted to be outside. She needed to feel Maine, not just be inside of it.

Since the snow had melted, we could go hiking.

We hadn't been to the top of Cadillac Mountain in months.

It was time.

The morning of our third day, I woke her at a little past three and asked her if she was feeling up to going hiking. She smiled so fucking big despite how early it was. And I saw the excitement on her face as she crawled out of bed. It only took her a few minutes to brush her teeth and get dressed.

It took me a little longer.

I had to make sure I had everything I needed.

With us being out of practice, our climb wasn't as polished as usual, and we reached the summit with only a few seconds to spare.

I wrapped my arm around her and pulled her against me as we sat on a rock on the east side, facing Schoodic Peninsula, and we watched the sun break above the water.

She didn't take her eyes off the horizon.

Mine didn't leave her.

"I love you," I said in her ear.

She nuzzled her cheek into my arm. "I love you, too."

For a long time, I'd known this woman was going to be my wife. I'd known I wanted to spend forever with her. That I wanted her to have my children.

Our relationship wasn't perfect, but we were strong.

Alix had accepted I would never be able to give her all of me while I was still working. Business would always hold the biggest stake in my life.

We could withstand that obstacle.

Along with the amount of time I would continue to spend at the office and the trips I made to the West Coast and the international ones that would be coming up as I opened an office in Europe.

And I had accepted that Alix would continue working as a paramedic until she got pregnant. She wasn't happy about the deal, so I suggested she become a dispatcher in the call center, work in an office, anything. I just didn't want my wife on the road where she could get harmed.

My wife.

That was a term I hadn't even considered before her.

But, in many ways, it was as though we were already married, living together, sharing a mortgage on our house here in Maine. She was the only person in this world who knew everything about me.

More than my parents and even my friends.

Alix couldn't say she didn't know the man she was marrying.

There weren't any secrets between us.

Well, except for one.

That was only because she didn't know about the ring I was holding in my hand, that I'd taken out of my pocket when we reached the top of the mountain.

I slid off the rock we were sitting on and moved in front of her, holding her hand, getting her onto her feet. While still clasping her fingers, I took a step back and got on one knee.

Her eyes widened as I gazed up at her. Her fingers squeezed my hand.

"Oh my God," she whispered.

She probably thought I hadn't heard her.

But I had. I saw the wonder in her eyes, and it matched the shock in her voice.

She was surprised, just the way I'd wanted her to be.

"Alix, I've loved you since the moment I saw you in the restaurant. When your bodyguard tried to stop me from writing my number on your hand."

Tears came into her eyes as she giggled from the memory.

"I want to spend the rest of my life with you. I want you to be my partner in every decision I have to make. I want you to promise me you'll be with me forever."

Tears streamed down her cheeks, and her bottom lip was quivering.

"What I'm going to promise you is, I'll never hurt you. I'll always take care of you and keep you safe. And I'll give you everything you've ever dreamed of." I kissed the top of her hand

and opened my fist, holding the ring against the tip of her finger. "I promise you forever."

"Dylan ..." she whispered, licking a tear off her lip.

I looked at the etched band and how each groove captured the light and then to the diamond and how the orange and pink from the sky was reflecting over it.

Finally, my stare moved to hers. "Will you be my wife?"

She nodded. "Yes. Of course."

I slid the ring onto her finger, and then I stood, pulling her into my arms. Her cheek pressed against my chest, and I held her face, so she couldn't move.

"I'm going to be your wife," she whispered into my jacket.

I released the back of her head and waited for her to look at me. Her expression caused me to smile. "Isn't that what you want?"

Her grin widened. "More than anything in this world."

FORTY

ALIX

PRESENT DAY

"GOOD MORNING, BABY."

My eyes flicked open.

I didn't move.

I didn't make a noise.

I just looked across the bed, the same way I did every morning.

I checked the pillow first.

Smith's head was resting on it, and the comforter wasn't any higher than his waist.

It had been his voice that had woken me.

Not Dylan's.

Last night was suddenly all coming back to me.

The sex.

The way I had fallen asleep in Smith's arms.

It explained why I was naked.

Why I felt sore.

Why I hadn't slept alone.

Smith wouldn't leave me.

All Dylan did was leave.

But Dylan hadn't had the opportunity to do that last night because I was here.

At Smith's.

And this was a moment.

One of the biggest ones yet.

There had been so many recently; it felt like all I'd been doing was celebrating.

"Alix ..."

Smith was trying to get me to look at him.

I hadn't made eye contact with him since I woke up.

I wasn't ready.

I didn't know how it would make me react.

But I couldn't keep avoiding it, especially since I'd been staring at his chest for what felt like a really long time.

I slowly lifted my stare.

And then our eyes connected.

The deepest green gazed back at me.

I wasn't sure I had even noticed his eye color before.

Now, it was all I saw.

It was so different than Dylan's blue.

So was his facial hair.

Dylan shaved every morning.

Smith had at least four days of scruff.

Dylan's hair was perfect when he got up.

Smith's was ruffled in a way that looked like fingers had been pulling it.

I guessed they had.

Oh God.

"Good morning," I replied, bringing the blanket up to my chin.

He was on his side, facing me.

Watching.

"You're not a morning person, are you?"

I thought about his question.

I actually considered myself as one.

But I certainly wasn't right now.

"Morning-ish," I said from behind the blanket.

"Does that mean you need coffee first?"

I had no idea what that meant.

But I knew I needed more than two seconds to process everything that was happening right now, and I was positive I couldn't do that with him in this bed.

"Coffee," I said, nodding.

His hand dipped beneath the covers.

His fingertips were on my leg.

Hip.

The center of my navel, brushing across my belly button.

It felt so good.

So did being here.

I was just waiting for the guilt to come, for it to slap me in the face, for it to cause my stomach to churn.

Because, once I really processed what I had done last night, it was going to fucking wreck me.

"Are you hungry?" he asked.

Smith's voice was so tender.

So was his touch, which was now back on my hip.

Once the guilt choked me, I would have a hard time keeping food down.

But one thing always stayed.

"I'll take the chocolate cake."

He laughed, showing me a smile that was overwhelmingly beautiful.

Like a sunny day.

"Just coffee and cake? Nothing else?"

"Nope."

He leaned forward and pressed his lips against the center of my forehead. "I'll be right back."

His cologne from yesterday still clung to his skin, giving me the warmest scent.

Warmth was what I'd felt the second his lips touched me.

Warmth was something I'd never had before.

Now, I couldn't imagine my life without it.

"Thank you," I whispered as he pulled away and climbed out of bed.

My eyes followed him to the closet, staring at the muscles in his thighs and the ones etched into his abs and arms.

His body was incredible.

And so was his dick.

As he walked out of the room, I couldn't stop replaying all the different ways he had pleasured me last night.

Even when Smith had pounded me with such an intense amount of strength, he had still been so gentle.

He was the opposite of Dylan.

I glanced at Smith's side of the bed.

I loved his dented pillow and how messy he'd left the blanket.

The only reason I looked away from it was because I heard his feet on the floor.

I sat up and brought the blanket with me, slipping my arms out, so I could grab the coffee and cake he handed to me.

As he climbed back into bed, I put a bite into my mouth and chewed. "Oh my God," I groaned. It was layered, just like the strawberry, and the cake was spongy with the richest flavor. "Tell me where you got this."

He pushed his back into the headboard and held his coffee mug against the mattress. Since he'd only put on a pair of sweat-pants, I once again had a close-up of his chest.

There was a sexy patch of thin, dark hair that covered the top of it.

Thick veins ran down his arms.

One of my favorite things was the small crinkles just to the sides of his eyes. They deepened when he smiled. He did so much of that when he was with me.

But he wasn't doing it now or when he said, "Roxbury."

I brought a clump of frosting up to my lips. "This could become my new go-to."

"I'll get you more the next time I'm there."

I glanced to my right, seeing him hold the glass to his lips. "Will you bring me?"

We'd had this conversation before.

He'd ignored me when I told him I wanted him to take me.

"Or I'll go without you," I added. "Just tell me the name of the bakery."

His brows pushed together. "You're not going there without me."

"Then, come."

He said nothing.

He didn't even take another sip of his coffee.

He just shut down.

That was the first time he'd done that in front of me.

"Smith, why don't you want me to go there?"

When he looked at me again, I saw something achingly familiar.

He had pain in his eyes that was identical to mine.

His fingers slid through his hair, and he tugged on the strands. "I'm protective of where I come from." He sighed. "I just don't want to hear the comments, and I don't want to be asked any questions."

"You think that's what I'd do?"

He was now holding the top of his head, and I could see the stress on his face. "What happened there didn't stay there, Alix. It haunts me every fucking day."

213

"I know what it's like to have nightmares. I have one every time it rains." I glared at the cake, unable to take another bite. "I know how scary it is. I know how you don't want to open your eyes. I know how helpless you feel. And I know what that dark pit of misery looks like and how tightly it can wrap its hands around your throat."

He was quiet again, looking toward the end of the bed.

He didn't move.

Until he finally glanced at me. "You're asking to see my storm."

I hadn't thought of it that way.

Or what that required of him.

And what that meant about us.

"Yes," I said so softly.

"I've never brought anyone there."

"Bring me."

I wasn't pleading.

I was making him a promise.

"Why do you want to go there, Alix?"

The bakery was an easy answer.

But it wasn't the real reason.

"I want you to show me that part of you," I answered. I moved the cake to the nightstand and rolled onto my side, so I could face him. "I really like you, Smith."

And I liked the way he treated me.

How he looked at me.

The way he cared for me.

"You want us?" he asked.

I could feel myself fitting in here.

In his life.

In his arms.

"Yes," I answered.

He reached over and brushed a piece of hair off my face. "I'm

214

going to take you to Roxbury." Then, his hand cupped my cheek. "I hope, one day, you'll show me your storm."

My heart began to throb in my chest.

My throat ached.

The guilt I'd expected to feel was for betraying Dylan by sleeping with Smith last night.

But what was gutting me was, I couldn't give Smith what he was asking for, so I looked away, unable to gaze into his eyes anymore.

He rolled onto his side and moved closer, pulling me into his arms. "I'll never push you." I relaxed a little as he hugged me against his body, rubbing his hands over my back. "Do you have to work tonight?"

"No."

"I might not let you go home."

Two nights away from Dylan.

I hated that I missed him.

FORTY-ONE

SMITH

PRESENT DAY

I PULLED up outside the police headquarters and parked along the curb. Since Alix had told me I wasn't able to go into her department, that having me in there would be violating HIPAA laws, I stayed in my car. Being that I was a few minutes early, I had time to take out my phone and go through some of my work emails.

I came across one from my assistant with the subject line: *Lake Tahoe.*

THE ROOM YOU ASKED ME TO LOOK INTO IS AVAILABLE FOR THE DATES YOU REQUESTED. I'VE ATTACHED THE ESTIMATED COST. THE FLIGHT INFORMATION FOR THE SAME DATES IS BELOW. LET ME KNOW IF YOU WOULD LIKE ME TO BOOK THEM.

I clicked on the file she'd attached and checked out the breakdown of the room. The hotel was at the base of the mountain, and the view was supposed to be incredible.

I was downloading some of the pictures the hotel had provided when Alix got into the car.

"Hi," she said just as I put my phone away.

She had on tight jeans and a hat, her hair in a braid that had fallen into the front of her tank top.

And that smile I loved was shining so fucking bright.

"You look gorgeous," I told her.

When she leaned toward me to give me a kiss, I inhaled the spiciness of her cinnamon scent. It made me so hard; I growled as I took her mouth against mine, holding her face for a few extra seconds.

As I released her, I asked, "Do you need to stop somewhere, or are we going straight to the restaurant?"

"We can head straight there." She took out her phone and looked at the screen. "Rose has already arrived. She texted me a few minutes ago."

I pulled onto the road and turned at the light, driving toward Copley.

This was the first time I would be meeting her best friend, and Alix had given me a warning this morning. She'd said Rose was protective and unfiltered.

She was Boston.

I knew that personality well.

And she was exactly who I would want Alix to be best friends with.

Handling her wouldn't be a problem.

When I got to the light, I put my hand on Alix's thigh and glanced at her. "I have something I want to talk to you about."

She looked nervous. "Okay."

I tightened my grip. "Is going to Lake Tahoe something you really want to do?"

"Yes," she answered immediately, and I saw the relief in her face. She had obviously thought I was going to bring up something else. "It's a place I'd love to see with you." Her hand went on top of mine, and she traced her nails up and down my fingers.

"I had my assistant look into some dates. I didn't know your schedule, so we can move things around if we need to. I just wanted to get a plan in place."

There was emotion in her eyes when she said, "You're so good to me."

I moved my hand to her chin, my thumb brushing along the bottom of her smile.

She deserved it.

She was just as good to me.

"I'll send you what she put together," I said. "And you can tell me if it works or not." The light turned green, and I looked back toward the road.

"Thank you."

"Of course, baby."

"I love when you call me that."

While I drove, I kept my hand on her face, fingers spread across her cheek and the dip of her neck, my thumb still grazing small patches of her skin. I got the sense she needed the comfort.

Alix, when are you going to tell me what happened to you?

Maybe what she needed was to see Roxbury from my point of view. To look at the different places and experience them through my eyes, my descriptions, my tumultuous memories.

It wouldn't be easy to bring her there.

But I had to do it.

I had to let her into that world, or she'd never fully understand me.

Reluctantly, when we reached the valet, I pulled away from her face and got out of the car. I met Alix on the sidewalk and wrapped my hand around hers, and she led me toward the outside seating area.

I saw Rose before we even got to her table. I could tell it was her by the way she was looking at us.

The differences between the two women immediately stood out.

I knew that from Rose's stare alone, from her posture, how she put herself together.

It was everything I had expected.

The girls hugged, and then Alix moved back and stood between us.

"Rose, this is him," she said.

The announcement almost sounded like a continuation of a conversation they'd had earlier, as though meeting me tied every-thing together.

Rose stuck her hand out for me to shake. "Hi, him."

I laughed. "It's nice to meet you, Rose."

We sat at the round table, and my hand found Alix's leg again, my thumb skimming the outside of her knee. Her smile was the reason I left it there and didn't pull it away.

A waitress came right over and asked if we wanted drinks.

"Three shots of Fireball," I told her.

"Anything else?" she asked.

"Three waters," I said.

The waitress looked at Alix, who said nothing, and then at Rose.

"I won't argue with that order," Rose said.

"It'll help get the awkwardness out of the way," I explained once the server left our table.

"I like how you roll," Rose admitted.

"Wait until I tell you about Lake Tahoe," Alix said, putting her hand on Rose's arm. "He's taking me there."

Rose's stare shifted over to me. "I'm impressed."

"That's not why I did it." My fingers slid to the inside of Alix's thigh. "You and I are on the same team; we only want what's best for this girl." I gazed at Alix as I spoke even though my words were intended for Rose. But what I was about to say

219

needed to be spoken directly to her, so I caught her eyes and said, "I won't ever hurt her; you've got my word."

Rose leaned into the edge of the table. "Just so you know, the man before you said the same thing."

"Rose," Alix hissed.

It was a warning.

One I hadn't missed.

"All I'm saying is, you're making me a promise that you might not be able to keep," Rose added.

I didn't care who had been in Alix's life prior to me.

I didn't care what he had promised.

He wasn't the man I was.

My stare intensified. The seriousness of what I was about to say took hold of my voice, and I gave her all the honesty I had when I said, "I want to be her sunny day."

There was a change in Rose's expression.

A softness.

Most wouldn't have seen it, but I had.

Slowly, she turned her attention to Alix and said, "I like him."

Maybe she didn't completely believe me.

But she would.

Because I was going to prove it to her.

FORTY-TWO

ALIX

PRESENT DAY

ABOUT A WEEK after we'd had dinner with Rose, which became the evening Smith had officially won over my best friend, he invited me to his office for lunch.

It hadn't been that long since I saw him.

I'd been to his place just two nights before, and I had stayed until the next morning.

Since Rose had mentioned the last man I'd been with hurt me, I expected Smith to ask about him. If he did, I wanted to be prepared with a story that was convincing, especially to someone who was used to dissecting lies for a living.

Telling him the truth wasn't an option.

Not if I wanted things to continue the way they were.

But what was reinforced even more during the days that followed was, Smith wasn't anything like Dylan. He didn't push. He didn't ask too many questions. He let me open at my own pace, and his patience was the reason I was letting him in deeper.

As for him, the moment I arrived at his office, I learned he was throwing me right into the darkness of his past when he looked up from his desk and said, "Are you up for having lunch in Roxbury?"

I circled my hands around the armrest of the chair and squeezed.

He was trusting me with his secrets.

It was a lot to process.

"Are you sure that's what you want?"

"That's really what I should be asking you," he said.

I no longer had to think about the answer to that question.

My feelings for Smith were so present, even on the nights I spent with Dylan.

"Yes," I said, "it's what I want."

He got up from the desk and waited for me to grab his hand before we walked through the reception area. We took the elevator to the parking garage and climbed into his car. He turned the music on low, the air-conditioning on high.

"Let me know if you get cold," he said, leaving the garage and turning onto the road.

"I won't." I looked at him. "You know that."

His expression told me he hadn't forgotten how much I loved the cold.

He was just being considerate.

Because he was the kind of man who was constantly concerned with what I needed.

And he proved that to me every time I was with him.

I reached across the seat and rested my hand on top of his.

I didn't bring attention to what I was doing.

I didn't say anything.

I just wanted him to know I was here.

To allow his thoughts to get where they needed to be, I stayed silent for most of the drive. I was so familiar with the route to Roxbury, so I knew how close we were getting. I'd taken this trip countless times, behind the wheel of an ambulance and as a passenger.

When we were a few blocks away, the environment began to change. There was more graffiti on the buildings, more trash piled on the sides of the street. People were camped out on the sidewalks, a grocery cart holding their belongings.

As we got off the main road and into the thickness of the neighborhood, I began to recognize many of the front doors. That was something I never forgot—the color, the handle, the style of the cutouts.

It was where medics would wait before we were let inside, what we stared at until it swung open.

"That's where I went to high school."

I looked at the brick building he was pointing at and read the sign that was engraved by the entrance.

It was one of the roughest high schools in Massachusetts.

I never would have guessed this gentle man had graduated from there.

"That was my first job," he said after he pulled back onto the street, and we were passing a convenience store. "I stocked the shelves. Three to six every morning with longer shifts on the weekends."

I knew the store well. I'd worked on several patients in the parking lot.

He turned left at an upcoming Stop sign, and after two blocks, he pulled over again.

He was silent.

I didn't look at him. I didn't want to give him that kind of pressure.

He'd talk once he was ready.

And, from experience, I knew how long that could take.

A heaviness filled the car.

I could feel the emotion every time I inhaled.

Not even the cold was helping.

The anxiousness was making my palms clammy, but I still clung to Smith's hand, refusing to let go.

"Right there."

I wasn't sure how much time had passed since he last said something.

Minutes probably.

But his voice was now haunted.

Gritty.

Hoarse.

Sounds I'd never heard from him before.

I followed his eyes to a duplex.

It was white. One story.

There were several other identical tenements next to it.

"We lived there the longest." His lids narrowed. "The window on the right was the room I shared with Star."

The glass was broken.

There was duct tape holding it together.

"There used to be a set of bloody handprints on the side of the rotted windowsill." His voice softened. "I'm sure they've lightened a lot, but I bet they're still there."

I stopped myself from asking questions.

He didn't need my inquiries.

Not at this moment.

Because, even though it was a clear day, it was raining inside his head.

The clouds were darkening.

It was on the verge of thundering.

"That's where it happened—the night my whole life changed."

I folded my fingers around his, waiting for him to continue.

"It was around three or four in the morning. I wasn't supposed to work a double, but I couldn't turn down the money when they asked me." The intensity in his gaze was harrowing. "The door to our room was locked when I got home. That wasn't unusual. I'd bought a lock with my very first paycheck, and I'd install it every time we moved. I didn't trust the junkies who were always at our place, shooting up with my mother." His hand had moved to the steering wheel, gripping it so hard that his fingers were almost white. "I didn't want to wake up Star by banging on the door, so I went outside to go in through the window. I was standing out there with my hands on the glass when I saw movement in the room." He breathed loudly, and the noise made me ache for him. "I don't think I even realized in that moment what he was doing to her. All I saw was Star. Her eyes. The way they were looking at me through the glass."

"Oh my God." I slapped my hand over my mouth, so I wouldn't say another word.

It was so hard to be silent.

So difficult not to wrap my arms around him and try to take some of his pain away.

I was a healer. I'd been one since I was a kid.

But nothing I said, nothing I did would repair him.

"I didn't even try to get the window open. I just balled up my fist and punched straight into the glass." I gazed at his knuckles and saw small scars marring his skin. "I tried to kill him, Alix." He looked at me, and I almost gasped from the torture in his eyes. "I put my hands around that motherfucker's throat, and I squeezed as hard as I could."

"He deserved it."

"He didn't die." He turned, gazing back at the house. "My sister screamed when she saw the blood all over me, and it woke a few of the guys who had been passed out in the living room. One of them ripped me off that motherfucker's throat. Back then, I wasn't strong enough to fight all three of them at the same time. But I did everything I could to get them out of my house." He

225

turned my hand over, putting it palm side up, and placed it on my leg. Slowly, his fingers rested on top of mine. "If those guys hadn't come in, I would have killed him." Our eyes locked. "I would have done anything to stop him from raping my sister."

"Did he go to jail?"

He shook his head. "Once they left, I never saw any of them again."

There wasn't a sound in the car.

I couldn't even hear us breathing.

We both just stared at the broken window.

It felt like someone had reached inside my chest and was strangling my heart.

I couldn't even imagine how Smith felt.

"I think about that moment every single day," he said. "What I could have done differently, what would have happened if I hadn't worked the double shift. If I had purchased a more expensive lock that couldn't be jimmied with a fucking roach clip."

God, I knew that feeling.

The things I asked myself were different yet so similar.

"It's all part of the precipitation—the wind, rain, the dark clouds," I told him. "Those questions all lead up to the storm."

"It won't ever stop."

"No."

"It won't lighten."

I shook my head. "No, it won't."

"I'm just going to have to face the thunder for the rest of my life."

At least he was facing it.

I was not.

"Has my past made you want to run?"

It was the most honest thing he'd asked since we got in his car.

I knew the story he'd just told wasn't his only demon.

226

I was sure the list of things he'd experienced was terrifyingly long.

That didn't make him a broken man.

It made him a hero.

Using both hands, I squeezed his palm and looked up. "No, I don't want to run. Unless it's toward you, and then my answer is yes."

FORTY-THREE

SMITH

PRESENT DAY

"NO, I don't want to run. Unless it's toward you, and then my answer is yes."

I stared at Alix while she sat in the passenger seat of my car, her words echoing inside my head.

By bringing her to Roxbury, I'd shown her a part of my storm.

But there was so much more.

I'd spent eighteen years in that hell. Every day was a war, another memory that would haunt me for the rest of my life. And each one had left me with scars. Time had lightened some. The rest were as dark as the black tar my mother shot into her veins.

Eventually, I would open my wounds and tell Alix the story behind them.

But, for now, I needed to clear my head.

I shifted into drive and put my hand on her thigh. "Do you have to work tonight?"

"No."

"I know I told you we were going to have lunch in Roxbury, but I can't. I'm sorry. I have to get the hell out of here."

She reached across the seat and put her hand behind my

head, her fingers running through the back of my hair. "I get it. You don't have to explain."

I appreciated that about her.

"You want to go to my place?" I asked.

"Don't you have to go back to work?"

I shook my head. "I had my assistant clear my schedule."

She smiled.

Fuck, I needed that.

"Then, yes, I would love to."

We passed the bakery I had gone to as a kid, but I didn't point it out to Alix. She'd want to stop, and I had other plans for dessert.

My idea was probably stupid.

But, the other day, I'd gone to the store and purchased everything I needed to make a cake. I didn't know what had caused me to grab the ingredients. I just knew I had been on my way home from Roxbury, and I'd needed something mindless to get my mother out of my head.

The same way I needed it right now.

I got us through the traffic and parked in my driveway, clinging my fingers around Alix's hand as I led us toward my front door. Once we were inside the kitchen, I lifted her into my arms and set her on top of the island.

She laughed as my hands moved to her knees. "It feels like you're about to feed me."

"I am." I slid her legs open and stepped between them. "But we have to make something first." I leaned forward, my lips gently pressing against hers.

"I'm starving," she said, her voice turning darker.

She wasn't just talking about food.

I fucking loved that.

"Let's get started." I went into the pantry, lifting the bags off the bottom shelf. On my way back, I took the milk and eggs out of the fridge and placed it all beside Alix.

I watched her look at the ingredients as I spread them over the counter and then again when I set the pan and mixer down as well.

"What is this all going to turn into?"

"A cake that can hopefully rival the ones you've had."

Her smile was so beautiful as I handed her the measuring cup and a bag of flour.

"I need two cups dumped in here." I pointed at the mixer.

"I'll ruin it."

She didn't cook.

She didn't bake either.

But she was going to learn, and I wanted to be the one to teach her.

"You're better than you think you are." Before she tried to protest, I added, "Trust me."

She looked away, and as she filled the cup, I dragged a knife across the top of the flour to even it out. Then, she dropped it into the mixer. Just as she began to refill again, the sun came through the window. It shined across the top of her hand, showing the tiny specks of flour that had stuck to her skin.

"Don't move."

She froze, her eyes questioning my command.

I took out my phone, snapping several pictures of her hand. I scrolled through the collection and picked the best one. "Look," I said, showing her the screen.

As she gazed at the phone, I dipped my finger into the flour and touched it to her palm, the same place I had just taken a picture of. My touch caused her to glance up, and she stared as I drew an S across her skin.

Once I finished, she reached into her purse that was wrapped diagonally across her body, and she removed her cell. "Don't move," she said with a grin, giving the order right back to me.

With my fingers still close to hers, she tapped the screen. When she finally pulled away, I watched her hit it several more times before a notification suddenly came across my phone.

It showed Alix had tagged me in a picture.

I opened the app and saw a photo of our hands with an S in the middle of hers. The sun was shining over us.

Underneath every shot she'd ever posted was a sun emoji.

Except for this one.

It had a red heart.

Our eyes locked.

She didn't need to say anything.

The picture had done the talking for her.

So had the tag and the symbol she'd used.

Today was a sunny day.

This fucking girl.

"Fuck this cake." My hands gripped her cheeks, and I slammed our mouths together, my tongue gliding in until I felt hers. "I need you right now."

My fingers lowered to her ass, and I pushed her closer to me until her legs wrapped around my waist. Once I had all of her weight, I walked us out of the kitchen.

"It was going to be chocolate, wasn't it?" she asked, her words vibrating across my lips.

I nipped her bottom one, sucking it into my mouth. "Do you really think I'd torture you with strawberry?"

Her laugh was different.

This time, it ended in a moan.

FORTY-FOUR

ALIX

PRESENT DAY

Me: I just got home from work.
Smith: Glad you got there safely. What time are you coming over?
Me: Probably around six. I'm going to throw some food down my throat, nap, then I'll be over.
Smith: Cake?
Me: It's like you're a mind reader or something.
Smith: I can't imagine how I came up with that.
Me: I bought a slice of strawberry. It's in my freezer. You're starting to wear off on me.
Smith: Bring it tonight. I'll eat it off you.
Me: I'm taking it out right now.
Smith: See you soon, baby.

———

Me: We're still on for tomorrow night?
Rose: Duh.
Rose: Wait, were you about to cancel on me? Because I haven't seen you in FIVE FUCKING DAYS.

Me: I'm not canceling. I'm just confirming. That way, when Smith tries to hold me hostage tomorrow night, I can tell him you have dibs.

Rose: That man really needs to learn how to share, and he also needs to stop making you so insanely happy. The amount you've been smiling lately is just disgusting.

Me: The nerve of him.

Rose: Seriously, I could not be happier for you right now. And I also miss you so incredibly much, it hurts.

Me: But you're getting me tomorrow night.

Rose: I cannot wait.

Rose: Hey, are you going over to Smith's tonight?

Me: I'm just getting dressed, and I'm going to head there in a few minutes. Why?

Rose: Alix ... it's about to rain.

I GLANCED up from the screen of my phone and rushed over to one of the windows.

I flipped open the blinds.

There was a dark sky above.

The leaves on the trees were blowing from the wind.

I looked at the street.

I could see the drops starting to make a puddle.

It wasn't coming down too hard.

That meant I had time.

I grabbed a sweater that had a hood and threw it on over my head. Leggings were yanked up my legs. My feet slid into sneakers, and I hurried down the stairs.

I lifted my purse off one of the barstools and took my keys out of the bowl in the entryway.

I walked out the front door.

Four steps left.

Three.

That was when I heard the noise.

The cracking.

The *craaack* that closed the back of my throat, preventing me from taking a breath.

The sound moved through my body like a vibration.

It felt as though my ears had exploded.

A headache stabbed through my skull.

My chest tightened.

My stomach ached.

I reached to my side, feeling all around for the banister. Once my fingers found it, I clung to the long pole, squeezing it with everything I had.

I tucked myself into a ball.

The coldness of the metal pressed into my face.

Rain splattered against my forehead.

It hit my cheeks.

It dusted my eyelashes.

I couldn't move.

I could only wait.

Bracing myself for the image that was about to plow through my mind.

The one that had started it all.

The one that had come with the same sound.

The one that would begin this ride.

And then I saw it.

The silence.

The darkness.

The *craaack*.

My purse fell from my arm.

My heart stopped.
And I no longer felt the rain.

FORTY-FIVE

SMITH

PRESENT DAY

I LOOKED DOWN at my phone and saw that it was six forty.

The last time I'd checked was just two minutes ago.

And then a minute before that.

Alix was late, and I knew it had everything to do with the weather.

It was fucking pouring outside. Thunder was blowing up the sky, and lightning was slashing across it.

I knew it was also the reason she hadn't responded to my texts or answered my calls.

The same thing had happened during the last storm.

It wasn't a coincidence.

I waited five minutes and called her again.

It rang four times, and then it went to voice mail.

I ran my hand through my hair, pacing my kitchen, trying to come up with a plan.

I couldn't go to her place.

I didn't know where she lived besides that it was somewhere in the Back Bay. That was the only thing she'd ever mentioned about her living situation. Whenever we hung out, she always came here. She never even invited me over.

I didn't push for it.

I didn't push her about anything.

And, because I hadn't, I had no control over what was happening tonight. No way to get in touch with her.

No way to help.

My gut told me she needed it, and I couldn't do a goddamn thing besides wait for her to call me back.

I pounded my fist against the countertop, causing my phone to jump. As it landed, a notification came across the screen that someone had liked the last photo I'd posted.

The same one Alix had liked.

An idea came to me.

I opened the app and went to the search bar where I typed in Rose's name. When her profile came up, I started a private message.

I hated that I had to reach out to Alix's best friend.

It wasn't my style at all.

But I had no other choice.

Me: It's Smith. Do you have a second to talk?

She replied almost immediately with her phone number.

I called, hearing her say, "Hey, Smith," after the first ring.

Rose had sounded so confident at dinner. All I heard now was concern.

"Sorry to reach out like this, but Alix was supposed to be here almost an hour ago. She's not returning my calls or texts. I'm wondering if you've heard from her."

"I sent her a message over an hour ago, and she hasn't written back."

I glanced out the window, seeing how hard it was still coming down. "Was that before the rain?"

She sighed. "The text was about the rain."

"The thunder has been going off every few minutes. I'm worried."

"I know." She paused. "But we won't hear from her until the storm is over."

Once the rain had started, I'd checked the weather.

The forecast made me even more concerned.

"It's supposed to rain until late tomorrow morning," I told her. "I can't wait that long to see if she's all right. I have to go check on her."

"Will you text me when you get there?"

I pressed my fingers into the side of my head, trying to ease the pounding. "That's why I reached out. I don't have her address."

"What do you mean?"

My hand dropped from my face, and it pushed against the counter. "I've never been to her place, Rose."

"Wait a second. Let me get this straight. You two have been together nonstop, and during that time, you've never once been to her townhouse?"

"No."

"Well, shit, I need to get to the bottom of that." I heard her say something to someone in the background, and when she returned to the phone, she asked, "What if Alix doesn't answer the door?"

"I'll break it down."

"Smith ..."

"There have been situations in my life that would have had a much better outcome had I arrived a few minutes earlier. Rose, I regret each one. I won't take that chance again, especially not with Alix."

"Jesus," she breathed into the phone. "I'll text you her address, and I'll meet you there in twenty minutes."

"See you then," I said and hung up.

I pulled the phone away from my face and looked at the screen. Rose's text came instantly, and I checked out the address.

All this fucking time, Alix had been living only eight blocks from me.

FORTY-SIX

ALIX

PRESENT DAY

COLD WAS what I felt across my entire body.

It went into my bones.

It made me shiver.

I was positive that was what I was doing.

And walking.

I was sure I was doing that, too.

At least, it felt as though my feet were moving over the pavement.

Like my sneakers were slipping a little from the wet tar.

The wetness was from the rain.

From the storm.

From the—

Craaack.

It was splattering against my forehead.

Hitting my cheeks.

Dusting my eyelashes.

It had to be.

But I no longer felt it, so I wasn't sure.

I felt nothing.

Except cold.

Craaack.

I clung to something.

It was hard, solid, even more freezing than the banister at my townhouse.

I had to hold on.

Because, while the memory filled my eyes, I couldn't be moving.

I couldn't be standing in the open air.

I had to have something in my hands.

Something touching me.

Protecting me.

And then it came.

Fast.

Hard.

And so fucking clear.

It was a snapshot.

A view made of millions of pixels.

I'd memorized them all.

Each one came with pain, like shrapnel slicing through my skin.

Just when I couldn't take another piece of metal, I was released.

Temporarily.

But it was enough time that I could be freed.

That I could feel the cold.

That I could feel the sidewalk as I moved down it.

But I couldn't feel my feet.

Or the rain on my forehead.

Or cheeks.

Or lashes.

This was the ride.

The one that wouldn't let me off until the sky stopped screaming.

I'd only ever experienced it inside my townhouse.

But, now, I was out here.

In the rain.

In the storm.

In the thunder.

Craaack.

FORTY-SEVEN
DYLAN
ONE YEAR AGO

"GOOD MORNING," I said, kissing my fiancée on the cheek as I set a cup of coffee in front of her.

I'd just returned from the bagel shop where I'd gotten us both poppy seed bagels with vegetable cream cheese and large coffees. I'd hoped to get back just as she was finishing her run, but the city was so busy; it had taken me triple the amount of time it should have.

"Morning," she responded, yawning, setting down the tablet she'd been reading from. She placed it next to the note I'd left her, telling her I was headed out to grab breakfast and coffee.

The screen of the tablet showed the home page of *The Boston Globe*. "Patriots' Day Celebrations" was the headline.

Alix had finished her forty-eight-hour shift at two this morning, and she'd been up before six. I'd tried to get her to stay in bed. But, with our wedding coming up in a month, she'd been logging extra miles on the days she didn't have to work.

She didn't need to exercise more. She had one of the best bodies I'd ever seen.

But running relieved her stress, and with the buildup of the holiday, the city had been crazier than normal.

I set the bagel in front of her and took a seat on the other side of the table. "What do you want to do today?"

"You're not working?"

I shook my head.

This was my first day off in three weeks.

I needed it.

And Alix needed it, too.

Now that I'd opened an office in London, I'd been working even more, flying back and forth several times a month. Our two-week honeymoon would be the longest I'd been away from the office in over a year.

Fourteen days of Alix.

No work.

No interruptions.

I couldn't fucking wait.

She lifted her coffee and held it to her lips. "Then, we certainly need to do something. I just don't know what since it's going to be pretty challenging to get around the city today."

I finished the first half of the bagel and wiped my mouth. "How about we go take a shower, head to the jewelers and pick up our wedding bands, and then we'll grab lunch and eat it at the Public Garden?"

She placed the coffee back on the table. "You never like to go to the park."

She was right.

It wasn't my favorite place.

But it was hers.

"It's beautiful outside," I said. "It'll be a good spot to eat and relax before we get caught in all the crazy shit that's happening around here today."

She smiled and took a bite. "I think that sounds like the

perfect afternoon." She glanced down at her hand. "I'm excited to see the way the bands came out."

Because Alix's engagement ring was so unique and Haifa had designed it himself, the wedding band had to be custom-made as well. We'd gone through the same process with mine, adding some etching into the black ring along with several diamonds.

"Four more weeks until you're mine."

She set the rest of her bagel on the table and stood, holding her coffee. "I'm already yours."

"I love when you say that," I growled.

She gave me the sexiest fucking smile and started walking out of the kitchen.

"Where are you going?"

"To take a shower," she said over her shoulder. "Come with me."

That was all I needed to hear.

I followed her upstairs and stripped my clothes off in the closet, meeting her in the bathroom. She was already standing under the spray, water splashing against her face. With her back to me, I circled my hands around her waist.

"God, you're beautiful." As I kissed her shoulder, my cock pressed into her ass, my fingers slowly sliding up until they were on her tits. "I want you to be my wife already."

She turned around, wrapping her arms around my neck, giving me a kiss. "In my eyes, I already am."

FORTY-EIGHT
SMITH
PRESENT DAY

ROSE WAS STANDING on the front steps when I arrived at Alix's townhouse. She was holding an umbrella over her head, shifting her weight between both legs, her arm wrapped around her stomach like it was aching.

Her body language told me whatever she was about to say wasn't going to be good.

And that was confirmed when I heard, "Alix isn't answering."

I held the hood over my head as I hurried up the steps to join her by the door. There was a large panel of glass in the middle, and as I looked through it, I saw there weren't any lights on.

I banged on the wood and jiggled the handle.

I didn't expect Alix to appear or for the lock to click open.

And it didn't.

"I'm trying not to panic," she said. "But I found this."

I turned my head to look at her.

She was holding Alix's phone.

"Where was it?" I asked.

"On the ground, just to the side of the steps, hidden behind the bushes. And there's more ..." She lifted her arm, showing me the purse hanging from it. "I found this, too."

My eyes shifted from the phone to the bag. "What the fuck does this mean, Rose?"

"I don't know."

"Alix wouldn't leave those outside." My heart was pounding so goddamn hard; I felt it in my ears. "Someone took her or she fell and was brought to the hospital or—"

"Let's not get ahead of ourselves. I've been in this situation with her before, and once the rain stops, I always hear from her."

"You mean, you've found her purse and phone on the ground before with no sign of Alix anywhere?"

"No. She usually just disappears and—"

"Fuck this, Rose. I'm calling the police."

I reached into my back pocket and took out my cell. Before my thumb even touched the screen, Rose's hand was on mine.

"Please don't call yet. Not until we've checked her house to know she's not inside. I know this sounds crazy, but Alix will literally kill me if we call nine-one-one."

"Then, open the door, so I can see if she's in there."

"I don't have a key."

I reached under my hood, tugging on my fucking hair. "I have to break the glass. I have no other choice."

She nodded. "Do it."

I tucked the sleeve of my jacket over my palm, trying to protect at least some of my hand, and I pulled my arm back. My fingers clenched into a fist. I eyed up the bottom-right corner, and I shot my hand forward, punching as hard as I could through the window.

Shards stabbed my skin.

The spiked edges of the glass scraped against me as I bent my wrist to reach the lock, opening the door from the inside.

The last time I had done this, I had been too late.

The motherfucker had already been raping my sister.

I didn't know what was happening to Alix, but I couldn't let anything or anyone hurt her.

I wouldn't survive it.

Not a second time.

Since Rose knew her way, I let her go in first, and I followed behind her. She flipped on the light in the entryway and rushed up the stairs and down a hallway.

"Alix?" Rose said as she walked into a bedroom I assumed was Alix's. "Are you in here?"

Except I didn't know why there was a man's button-down hanging over the corner of the chair or why there was a large pair of black leather lace-up shoes on the floor next to the ottoman.

"Is this her room?" I asked.

There was no sign of Alix in here, and Rose didn't answer me. She just moved through the room and went inside what looked like a walk-in closet.

"Oh my God," Rose gasped.

She'd found her.

I hurried over and saw Rose in the center, holding the top of the island with both hands.

But, as I skimmed the space, I didn't see Alix.

All I saw were clothes.

And most of them were for a man.

"Whose closet is this?" I asked.

Her skin was turning pale.

"Rose, what's going on?"

She backed up to the section where the entire rack had broken. The suits it had been holding were on the floor in a massive pile. The metal pole the hangers had been on was to the side of the large heap. She knelt, running her hand over a jacket and pulling it into her arms. "Oh, Alix, why didn't you tell me?"

Her voice was so fucking quiet.

I didn't like it.

Because Rose knew what was happening in here, and I was in the fucking dark.

"Tell me what the hell I'm looking at," I insisted.

She got up and moved over to one of the shelves that held several pairs of women's heels. There was a small piece of paper resting on the wood, which she lifted into her hand and read whatever was on it.

"Oh God," she groaned. She took a few more steps and stopped by a section of men's belts. "I can't believe this."

I turned, so I could see what she was staring at. There was a note taped to the wall.

The handwriting wasn't Alix's.

I'LL TRY NOT TO BE LATE.
I LOVE YOU.

There were tears in Rose's eyes. They were dripping down her cheeks.

And the expression on her face was scaring the shit out of me.

She hadn't said anything that made sense.

She hadn't given me a single goddamn clue of where Alix might be.

The patience I normally had was gone.

"I'm calling the police," I said, reaching for my phone again.

"Just give me another minute," she pleaded. "I need to check a few more things, and then you can do whatever you want." She moved by me and went back into the bedroom and out into the hallway. She called out, "Alix," as she checked the other rooms up here.

There was no response.

When I followed her downstairs, she flipped on another light, and it illuminated the whole kitchen.

As soon as Rose saw the space, she gasped and cried, "Oh God, no."

I looked around to see what had upset her.

The only thing I could come up with were the small pieces of paper that were everywhere—on the counters, taped to the cabinets, spread out across the table.

There was a briefcase on one of the barstools.

A jacket was resting on the back of one of the chairs. It was far too big to fit Alix.

I went over to it and saw it had an Embassy Jets logo on the left side of the chest.

And then I noticed the note that was right in front of it.

It had the same handwriting as the one on the wall in the closet.

I'm headed out to grab breakfast and coffee.
See you after your run.
I love you.

"Smith ..."

I glanced up.

Rose was standing at the counter not far from the table. She'd set Alix's purse on top of the granite, and next to that was a phone.

Alix's cell case was yellow.

This one was black.

Rose's arms crossed over her chest, and she looked like she was going to be sick. "It's been over a year since I've been in here. I didn't realize it had been that long. It didn't even dawn on me until we were up in her room." She swallowed, flattening her hand against her heart. "I've picked her up here, and I've talked to her outside on the front steps, but I've never come in."

"Why are you telling me this?"

She shook her head. "I didn't know this was happening, Smith." She broke eye contact, and I tracked her stare to the cabinets and countertop. "How did I not know?" When she faced the front again, she gazed at Alix's purse and dipped her hand inside, pulling out a ring.

A diamond ring.

What the fuck?

"Oh, honey," she sobbed.

She wasn't talking to me.

She was speaking as though Alix were here.

She touched the screen of the black-cased phone and whispered, "It's Dylan's ..."

I couldn't take another goddamn second of this.

I was standing in a home Alix obviously shared with another man.

One there was no way she could afford on her salary.

Rose was holding Alix's ring.

The whole goddamn time, she'd been engaged.

This was the reason she never invited me over.

This was what Alix didn't want me to see.

"Rose?"

Her eyes finally flitted to me. There were so many emotions staring back; I wasn't sure which was more dominant, but all of them made my chest pound.

"Who the fuck is Dylan? What is going on? And why isn't Alix in this goddamn house?"

"She told me not to bring up Dylan at dinner." Her head dropped, and her shoulders rounded. "Now, it all makes sense."

I was trying to piece together the few things she'd said. "What does?"

She set the ring on the counter and moved closer to me. "I need you to trust me for just a few more minutes. And then I promise I'll explain everything to you." She was headed toward the door.

"Where are you going?"

When she turned around, her eyes were so fucking haunted. "I think I know where she is." Just as I opened my mouth to respond, she cut me off and said, "You have to come with me, Smith. She needs you."

FORTY-NINE

ALIX

PRESENT DAY

I HURT.

My feet.

Legs.

My stomach from shivering.

Even my skin from the sopping wet clothes that clung to me.

They were so heavy.

Everything inside me felt unbearably heavy.

And each step caused the fabric to chafe.

It would only get worse.

Because it was still raining.

There was so much water.

So much wind, too.

And then ...

Out of nowhere ...

Craaack.

The pain was too strong.

I couldn't take another step.

I couldn't go on.

This was where I'd ended up, wherever this was.

I pushed myself to the right, not knowing what was waiting for me there.

And, when my body hit something hard, I gripped it.

It was cold metal.

It hugged me.

Squeezed me back.

That was what I needed, what I'd been searching for this whole time.

When my lids started to get heavy, they closed until I heard, "Alix," and then they snapped back open.

It was Dylan's voice.

Where is he?

I looked up.

Down.

To my right and left.

He wasn't there.

Because he was in front of me.

On the other side of the metal.

I didn't know what he was doing here.

But he was just a few feet away.

And my eyes landed on him.

And ...

"Oh my God," I choked.

My hand slapped over my mouth.

My chest heaved.

He was so incredibly handsome.

So much so that it hurt.

And it hurt even more than the pain I was already feeling.

I studied his face.

His cheeks were bare of any scruff.

His hair was perfectly gelled.

He was so polished.

He was waving at me, signaling me to come closer.

So, I released the metal, hearing it click as I opened the latch and moved through the opening.

My toes burned after each step.

My thighs throbbed.

He was farther away than I'd thought.

Up and up and up.

And down, down, down.

Up.

Down.

And then I saw him.

He was on the grass.

I was almost out of breath when I reached him, sitting on the ground directly in front of him. "Hi." I smiled. It made me feel warmth, like it was heating my skin through the rain. "What are you doing out here?"

His hand went to my chin. "My Alix."

I smelled his spicy scent.

Felt his freezing skin.

"I miss you," he said.

Why do those words hurt so badly?

Why can't I catch my breath?

Why, when I go to say them back, aren't I able to?

Because my mouth was already open, and rain was splashing against my lips and tongue.

I put my hand on my chest to stop the pain.

But what ached the most was the feeling that had come over me.

The one that made me want to close my eyes.

"I'm tired," I admitted.

"I know."

"Dylan, I'm so, so tired."

"I can tell."

Dylan blue. That was the color I called his eyes.

And that was what was finally staring back at me.

For so long, I hadn't looked.

I couldn't.

But, now that I did, it hurt.

Oh God, did it hurt.

"I can't keep doing this." I tucked my knees against my chest and wrapped my arms around them. "I can't keep fighting for us."

"I know, Alix."

My eyes were so heavy; I could barely keep them open.

"I don't think I'm going to make it up to bed tonight," I said. "I just don't have it in me."

His hand lifted to my cheek. "You don't have to, my love."

I stretched my body across the grass, smelling the wet soil beneath me.

My knees moved to my chest again.

I used my arm as a pillow.

I looked across the grass, like I would when I checked our bed.

There was no dented pillow.

There was no tousled blanket.

"Don't leave until I fall asleep," I told him.

Rain pounded against my ear.

Wet hair stuck to my cheeks.

"I'm going to stay with you," he said.

I felt heat behind me.

I felt more around my stomach.

He was holding me.

And, just when I expected him to wish me a good night, tell me he loved me, promise me I wouldn't freeze in the cold, I heard something else.

Craaack.

FIFTY

DYLAN

ONE YEAR AGO

AFTER A LATE LUNCH in the Public Garden, Alix and I left the park and began heading home. Her hand was in mine, and our two wedding bands were in my pocket. Rings that would be on our fingers in just a month's time.

Jewelry I'd never take off.

Not even to shower.

Being that we were so close to the wedding, I'd gone ahead and made several financial decisions. Alix had been added to the deed of my townhouse and was now the beneficiary to all of my personal accounts.

I'd told her the news a few weeks ago.

Her reaction had been exactly what I had expected.

It just wasn't important to her.

But it was to me.

These decisions would affect her future.

The same way turning down Arlington Street and then Boylston Street would affect mine.

It was two thirty in the afternoon.

The sidewalks were congested.

The city was buzzing with energy.

And something was leading me to Copley Square.

The finish line.

Alix didn't even ask where we were going.

She didn't have to.

She knew me well enough to already know.

I looked at her just as we were making the right, when it was clear I wasn't taking her home.

She was smiling out of the corner of her mouth and said, "I knew this was where we'd end up today."

I grinned back at her.

Taking her here wasn't just for me.

It was also for her.

She loved this city.

Since it was Patriots' Day, that gave us all the more reason to be in the heart of it.

And, today, the heart was Copley Square.

"Alix," someone said as we reached the corner of Dartmouth Street.

She stopped and looked for the person who had spoken her name.

It was a police officer.

He was standing at the Stop sign, and Alix released my hand to approach him.

"Hey, Charlie," she said as her arms wrapped around him. "It's so nice to see you." She pulled away and moved between us. "Charlie, this is my fiancé, Dylan Cole."

"Nice to meet you," the officer said as he shook my hand.

I wasn't surprised Alix knew him.

The police worked closely with the paramedics.

Whenever we were at a public event like this one, she always knew several of the officers on duty.

"Likewise," I replied to the officer.

Our hands separated, and he turned his attention to Alix. "How did you get out of working today?"

"I worked it last year. Our department rotates holidays, so we don't have the same one year after year."

"Lucky." He winked. "It's good to see you." He glanced at me. "You, too, Dylan."

Alix patted him on the shoulder. "Keep us safe today."

"You bet."

Her fingers found mine, and we continued walking until we reached the section where the flags were flying, the ones that represented all the countries participating in the race.

We found a place against the metal barricade that blocked us from entering the road.

The people around us were cheering.

They were holding signs and snapping photos of every runner who made it to the end.

I glanced at Alix.

It was like the morning we had hiked to the top of Cadillac Mountain for the first time, and I'd watched the sunrise through her eyes.

That was what I was doing now as she took it all in.

I'd spent my whole life in this city.

I'd stood in this same spot on this holiday every year since I was a kid.

And what filled me was a sense of pride.

People traveled from all over the world to come here.

To watch this race.

To experience this moment.

And, now that we were here, I felt something.

I didn't know what it was or how to describe it.

It was just an overwhelming sense of urgency that had me reach into my pocket at two forty that afternoon and take a ten-dollar bill out of my wallet.

I folded the money and put it in Alix's hand. "Do you mind going to get us some water?" I knew the street so well; therefore, I knew, "There's a store on the next block."

It wasn't hot.

I wasn't thirsty.

She laughed and stood on her tiptoes to kiss me on the cheek. "Of course. I'll be right back."

She turned, and I grabbed her hand, forcing her to look at me. "I love you, Alix."

She was still smiling. "I love you, too."

I released her.

And I watched her walk away.

As I stared at her back, I thought about moments.

The ones I'd spent with Alix.

The ones before her.

How I'd never really taken the time to celebrate any of them.

But the people standing on both sides of me were doing plenty of that.

They were celebrating this moment.

So, I did, too.

I closed my eyes and reached my hand into my pocket, feeling the small velvet pouch that held both wedding bands.

I squeezed it against my palm.

I didn't know why.

I just knew I had to.

And I thought of Alix.

I pictured her face when I'd placed the engagement ring on her finger. Her expression when I'd promised I would never hurt her, that I would always take care of her and keep her safe, that I'd give her everything she'd ever dreamed of. The look in her eyes when I'd promised her forever.

Nine minutes had passed since I sent Alix away.

And, now, another moment was happening.

One that caused me to break every promise I'd made to her.

Except for one.

Before I was able to do anything—take a breath, open my mouth, or turn my head to look in the direction of where Alix was —my entire life changed.

Alix's life changed.

Boston changed.

Forever.

FIFTY-ONE

ALIX

ONE YEAR AGO

WHEN IT WAS MY TURN, I walked up to the register, setting the two bottles of water and the bag of gummy worms on the counter.

"Did you find everything you needed?" the salesclerk asked. He was an older gentleman with an accent that told me he was from the area.

"I did," I said. "Thank you."

While he rang up my items, I flicked the edge of the money against the pad of my thumb, anxious to get back outside.

He looked at me over his glasses. "Have you been here all day?"

I shook my head. "We just got here."

"Before my shift, I got to see the winner cross the finish line. Took him just over two hours. Unbelievable to watch."

"Such talent. I bet it was beautiful to see."

I gave him the ten when the amount was totaled on the screen.

"Enjoy yourself out there," he said, and then he moved on to the next customer.

I tucked the waters under one arm and used both hands to open the bag of candy, popping a few worms into my mouth as I stepped out of the store.

When I'd woken up this morning, I'd had a feeling that Dylan and I would end up at the marathon today. We hadn't discussed it, but once I'd heard his plans didn't extend beyond lunch, I had known we'd head here after.

Despite the crowds and chaos, it was impossible to stay away.

There was too much camaraderie.

Energy.

The optimism was contagious.

Everyone—from children to the elderly—wore smiles.

Every year, the city would come together and welcome and encourage and cheer on these runners, and it was a sight one could never grow tired of.

Including us.

As I got closer to where Dylan was standing, I saw the flags waving in the wind. The giant digital clock that kept the time for the race was ticking away. Glitter was all over the ground from the poster boards people were holding in the air.

I took another mouthful of worms, and just as I was walking past the cross street, a noise blasted through my ears.

It was a sound I'd never heard before.

A *craaack* that shook my entire body.

It reminded me of thunder.

As though the sky had opened up and was whipping the air directly in front of me.

The waters dropped from my arm.

The bag of candy fell from my hand.

I swallowed what was in my mouth even though it had been barely chewed, and my hands went over my ears, cupping them to stop my eardrums from exploding.

I was on the ground.

My body in a tight ball.

My forearms and elbows shielding my face.

There was smoke.

Dust.

Tiny pieces of something sharp pierced into my knees and shins.

I let go of my ears to hold the ground, and there was an eerie silence.

Everything was still.

For one second, two seconds.

And then I heard the wails.

It was the sound a parent would make if they found out their child had passed away.

A scream that had come straight from the gut.

And it was coming out of me.

My nails dug into the pavement. My sneakers scraped across the tar as I tried to push myself forward.

There was only one thought in my head.

Dylan.

I had to get to him.

I had to see if he was okay.

I had to find out what the fuck was happening.

What had caused the thunder, the screams, the blood.

Because it was everywhere.

Darkening the skin on my hands as I dragged myself to the spot where we had been standing. Spreading across my knees as they skimmed the ground. Dripping down my forearms each time I fell and pulled myself back up.

I crawled.

Over people.

Over pools of blood.

My chin hit the asphalt as my hands gave out, and I tasted sand.

Rocks crunched between my teeth.

Blood spurted against the roof of my mouth when I bit my tongue.

Something grabbed ahold of my leg, and I kicked it until it let go, getting myself back on my knees so that I could keep moving.

I crept past clothes.

A finger.

Severed limbs I had to launch my body over.

But I kept going.

Kept screaming.

Kept shouting, "Dylan!"

I didn't know if he could hear me.

The smoke was making it hard to see.

Hard to breathe.

Hard to think about what I was supposed to do.

Everyone I saw needed my help.

But I couldn't stop for them.

I needed to find Dylan.

So, I dragged my body toward the flags.

Most of them were ripped.

Many of them were missing.

But I saw the broken poles and the tattered fabric, and I crawled toward them.

"Dylan!"

My fingers stuck together from all the blood.

Something new was stabbing the center of my palm.

Something hard fell onto my back.

It didn't slow me down.

Because, through the tiny cracks I was weaving between, I saw Dylan's black jacket. The white logo on the breast pocket. Dangling from the sleeves were two familiar hands that I had just been holding a few minutes ago.

He was on the ground.

"Dylan!"

I didn't know if my feet could hold me, so I stayed on my knees. I kicked, and I pushed.

And I crawled.

And I only let myself stop when I reached him.

My hands slid underneath his shoulders, and I pulled him onto my lap.

My fingers then pressed into his neck to find his pulse.

I couldn't breathe.

I could only scream.

And yell, "Dylan," over and over.

When I felt nothing, my arms wrapped around him while his back pressed against my chest.

I rocked.

And I cried.

And I shifted forward and back, repeating the pattern as though the movement could shock his heart into rhythm.

Spit flew from my lips.

Tears ran from my cheeks.

Blood dripped onto his face as my mouth rested on his forehead.

"Dylan."

I held him so tightly.

I didn't want him to be cold.

I didn't want him to hurt.

I just wanted him to know I was here.

"Dylan ..."

Just as I got his name out again, I felt something.

It was in my chest.

Like a bear clawing out of his den after months of hibernating.

It caused my neck to lean back.

My mouth to open.

My eyes to look at the sun.
A scream came out first.
It filled my ears.
Not as loud as the thunder.
But close.
And then I saw something drifting from the sky.
It hit my forehead.
My cheeks.
It dusted my eyelashes.
And I knew what it meant.
When ashes fall ...
That was the end.

FIFTY-TWO

ALIX

ELEVEN MONTHS AGO

"WE NEED to talk about your eating," Rose said from the other side of the table. "I'm really starting to get worried."

I glanced down at the spot in front of me.

There was a paper placemat and an empty wine glass.

In front of Rose was a basket, which had held a burger and fries that she'd devoured after the first round of drinks.

I took my hand off my lap and reached for the glass, twirling the stem between two of my bandaged fingers.

There were several more bandages on my palms and forearms.

My knees.

Shins.

I was on my second round of antibiotics.

I'd probably need a third.

"I eat," I told her. "Stop worrying."

"What? Celery?"

While she'd been inhaling her dinner, a small sliver of a fry had fallen out of the basket.

It was now on the table.

268

The sight of it made my stomach churn.

My mouth watered.

I had to look away before I threw up.

In the last month, I hadn't been keeping much down.

I knew that needed to change.

My weight was even starting to scare me.

Before I had a chance to reply, the waitress came to our table and dropped the leather check holder in front of me that held the receipt and my credit card. "I saw your name on the card," she said.

I looked up at her. "Okay."

Her hand shot through the air, and I watched every inch her fingers moved until they landed on my shoulder.

I stiffened.

She widened her grip, her thumb rubbing back and forth. "I saw your picture online. What that bomber did ..." Her voice trailed off as tears filled her eyes. "Anyway, I just wanted to say I'm sorry and to thank you for the service you've given to this city."

She left the table, not waiting for a response.

And I sat there, staring at Rose, wishing there were another full glass of wine in front of me.

"I can't escape," I whispered.

A picture of me had been aired on every news outlet across the country. It wasn't a close-up. It was a wide shot that showed the entire area around the finish line. The metal barricade had blown down, and I had crawled over it, holding Dylan in the road.

I was rocking him.

My lips were pressed to his forehead.

His hand was resting over my arm.

In the description, my name and occupation had been mentioned.

And, since then, my social media accounts had been gaining so many new followers every day. I was getting recognized on the streets. Flowers were being sent to the fire station, which the chief dropped off at my townhouse once a week.

Boston was supporting me.

I just didn't want the attention.

"It will eventually quiet down," Rose said. "It's just still so fresh right now."

As fresh as the wounds on my hands.

And the ones inside my mind that hadn't even begun to heal.

Because all I did day after day was replay it in my head.

Like I was doing now.

I had to get out of here.

"I'm going to go," I said, standing from my chair, slipping my purse over my shoulder.

"I'll walk you home."

I shook my head. "I'm fine. I promise." I moved over to her, hugging her as tightly as I could, knowing it wasn't even half as hard as she was squeezing me. "I'll text you when I get home."

"You'd better." She sighed. "Can I see you in a few days?"

I released her and nodded.

I'd probably cancel.

But, for now, I didn't need Rose nagging me, and the nod would keep her off my back for at least a day or two.

"Love you," I said over my shoulder as I started walking down the sidewalk.

"Love you more."

I took a few more steps and turned down the cross street.

Fortunately, the restaurant Rose had chosen wasn't far from my townhouse. She had done that on purpose. She didn't want me going more than a couple of blocks.

As though the extra walking would hurt me more.

Ironically, it was one of the few things that didn't hurt.

When I got onto my block, my speed increased, and I hurried up the steps.

I counted each one.

I wasn't sure why; it just made me feel better.

I unlocked the door and went inside.

Instead of putting my keys in my purse, I stuck them in a bowl on a table in the entryway.

It was decorative, not for storage.

I didn't give a fuck.

Normally, I carried my bag upstairs and left it in the closet.

But it felt so heavy.

So, I set it on the closest barstool in the kitchen.

Right in front of it, on the counter, was a note from Dylan.

I had eighty-four notes from him.

That was how many I'd saved.

As I read his words, I grabbed the bottle of red and poured myself a glass that I carried to the stairs. I was so tired; I barely had the energy to climb them.

Once I was inside my closet, I dumped my earrings and watch in a drawer, my clothes went in the hamper, and my shoes stayed wherever they'd landed on the floor.

Too exhausted to brush my teeth or wash off the tiny bit of mascara I'd actually put on, I brought the wine over to the bed, and I slid in. As soon as I found a comfortable spot, I pressed a button on the tablet that flipped off the lights and another that turned on the TV.

HGTV.

That was the only channel I could tolerate.

One I knew that would never mention the bombing.

I took a few sips of wine and sank into the mattress, my muscles slowly starting to relax.

The warmth from the alcohol moved toward the center of my chest. I set the glass on the nightstand and pushed myself down until my head was nestled into the fluffy pillow.

My eyes closed.

I rolled onto my stomach.

Just as I was hugging a pillow against my side, I heard the door open.

My eyes burst open.

I stopped breathing.

My body began to shake.

I couldn't take another wound.

I couldn't handle more trauma.

This was the end.

And I was already at it.

Whoever had just entered my bedroom, I hoped they killed me before they inflicted any pain.

I would rather die than feel worse than I did right now.

Just as I went to turn around to meet the face of the intruder, I heard, "It's me."

Dylan.

Oh God.

I didn't know whether to cry or celebrate.

Or put my hands on the sides of my head and shout, "How?"

I didn't do any of those things.

I stayed as calm as I could and said, "What are you doing here?"

So much of me wanted to turn around and look at his handsome face.

But I couldn't.

The agony was too intense.

For now, his voice was enough.

"I miss you."

My hand slapped over my mouth as a sob exploded from my lips.

The ache in my chest was unbearable.

I couldn't take another second of it.

"Don't," I cried. "Dylan, please don't."

I immediately regretted saying that to him.

I wanted him to miss me.

I just couldn't hear it.

"You went out tonight?"

The guilt.

It was coming up from my stomach and working its way into my mouth.

It had the flavor of bile.

"Yes," I answered.

"That's what I want," I heard him say. "Because tonight was a moment. Just like yesterday was and the day before that. Every milestone, every victory, I want you celebrating each one, Alix."

Rose would like this suggestion.

She was down for celebrating anything, especially if it meant progress. It would give her something to concentrate on, so she would stop worrying about me every second.

"Can you do that for me?"

"I can try," I answered, shaking my head to make sure I was hearing this all correctly.

"Promise me, Alix."

I squeezed the pillow with both hands. "I promise."

"Then, I'm going to say good night."

"No!" Something was tightening in the back of my throat, and I could barely swallow. "Don't go."

I felt a heat move behind me.

I felt more slip across my stomach.

He put his arm around me and a calmness came into my body.

"Good night," I whispered.

Before I fell asleep, I replayed it.

Every second.

Every detail.

And I stored it all.

Because, even though tomorrow was a new day, it was going to look exactly like today.

But that might be okay, especially if that meant Dylan would come home.

FIFTY-THREE

SMITH

PRESENT DAY

THREE AND A HALF MILES.

That was how far Rose and I were going in hopes that we would find Alix.

I stared at the screen of my phone, watching the route the driver took, counting down the seconds until we arrived.

I just needed to know she was safe.

Or I needed to get the police involved.

But this unknown was making everything inside me fucking ache.

During the drive, Rose explained what I had seen back at Alix's.

She broke down each layer.

I wished they were things Alix had told me.

That she had let me in deeper, allowing me to see what triggered her. Why she disappeared every time there was a storm. How the intensity of her PTSD swallowed her every day.

I understood why she hadn't told me.

Trauma wasn't easy to discuss.

I knew that firsthand.

But mine had happened years ago, whereas Alix's was still so fresh.

Time would eventually tame her demons. They would still be there. They would be there for the rest of her life. But the fangs of those demons would dull, and so would its claws.

Knowing the driver was about to pull over, I looked out the window and said to Rose, "You really think she's here?"

I didn't doubt her knowledge.

Rose certainly knew Alix better than I did.

But this was a hell of a walk from Alix's townhouse. It was fucking pouring. She had no cell and no purse, so going by foot was basically her only option.

"If she's not here, we're calling the police," she said. "And then I'll start freaking out for a whole different set of reasons."

I slid my hood over my head and opened the door, pushing myself out of the car. I waited for Rose and shut it behind her, and then I went with her to the entrance. She lifted the latch to let us into the gate.

As she led us down the paved walkway, the only sound was the rain.

I was lost in too many thoughts to talk.

The same amount of questions was swirling through my goddamn head.

To try to get them to settle a little, I focused on my steps and how this walk seemed so fucking endless.

The ground wasn't flat.

We climbed several hills and made a few turns.

And, when we reached a spot that was high enough to overlook the rest of the land that was inside the massive gate, Rose's arm shot into the air, and she said, "She's there."

I looked at where she was pointing.

The fog that had formed over the lower points made it hard to see anything. But, after a few seconds, it lifted, and I was able to make out a body on the ground.

I didn't waste a fucking second.

I took off running as fast as I could.

As I got closer, I saw the outline of her body. She'd tucked her knees against her chest, and her head was resting on her arm as though it were a pillow.

My feet pounded on the pavement, closing the distance between us.

Once I reached her, I fell onto my knees and put my hands on her back. "Baby?"

She didn't move, not even when I shook her.

And she didn't say a word.

Goddamn it, Alix, come back to me.

I put my hands under her arms and pulled her out of the ball. I dragged her against my chest, holding her like a baby. "Alix, can you hear me?"

Rain poured on us both.

Thunder was cracking directly above us.

Her skin was ice.

Her pulse was slow.

She was sopping wet.

"You're going to be okay," I told her.

As I brought her in closer, I looked at the headstone that was right in front of me.

DYLAN COLE
1980–2013
"WISHING FOR A SUNNY DAY ..."

"You're going to get a sunny day," I whispered in her ear. "Just hang in there."

My arm went under the backs of her knees, and I lifted her

into the air. When I turned around, Rose was only a few feet away.

"Is she okay?" she asked, panting.

"She has a pulse, and she's breathing; she's just not responding to me."

Rose took out her phone and said, "I'm calling nine-one-one right now. Do you want to bring Alix to the entrance, so it'll be easier for the paramedics to find us?"

I was already on my way, carrying her through the storm, hoping the warmth from my skin would do something to help her.

She didn't stir the entire walk back to the entrance.

She didn't let out a single moan.

Not even when I brought her to the ambulance and set her on the stretcher.

"What hospital are you taking her to?" I asked as I stood by the double doors.

I watched as the medics began to hook her up to machines, calling out numbers that meant nothing to me.

"Mass General," one of them replied.

"I'm going with her," Rose said, her fingers now on my arm. "And don't try to fight me on it because I will win that battle." She was now pulling my arm. "Look over there. I got you a cab, and you're going to follow us to the hospital."

When I finally took my eyes off Alix, I saw what Rose was talking about.

There was a taxi pulled up to the curb, waiting for me.

"Don't take your eyes off of her."

"I won't," she promised.

I climbed into the taxi, telling the driver to follow the ambulance, and he stayed directly behind it the entire drive. Once I arrived at the hospital, I found Rose, and we were put in a waiting room in the emergency department.

A nurse came in to treat my hand since I wouldn't go into an exam room.

I didn't care that I was still bleeding from the glass. I wasn't leaving this spot until I knew what was happening with Alix.

After I was glued and bandaged, I sat in the chair and didn't say a word.

Neither did she.

The only movement I made was when I reached into my pocket and took out my phone, typing Alix's name into the search engine.

The first article that came up was from *The Boston Globe*.

I clicked on it.

BOSTON MARATHON BOMBING: THE SURVIVORS
BY DAWN WARREN
APRIL 16, 2013
BOSTON RESIDENT ALIX RAYNE, 28, A PARAMEDIC FOR BOSTON EMERGENCY MEDICAL SERVICES, WAS LOCATED NEAR THE FINISH LINE ON BOYLSTON STREET, DIRECTLY OUTSIDE COPLEY SQUARE, WHEN BROTHERS, DZHOKHAR TSARNAEV AND TAMERLAN TSARNAEV, DETONATED THEIR TWO PRESSURE COOKER BOMBS.
RAYNE WASN'T IN THE AFFECTED AREA DURING THE EXPLOSION BUT WAS ON HER WAY BACK TO IT TO JOIN HER FIANCÉ, DYLAN COLE, 33, OWNER OF EMBASSY JETS. THE EXPLOSION SENT RAYNE TO HER KNEES, AND ONE WITNESS DESCRIBES SEEING HER CRAWL TOWARD THE BLAST SITE. WHEN RAYNE FOUND COLE, WHO HAD BEEN BLOWN MORE THAN TWENTY FEET AWAY FROM WHERE HE HAD BEEN STANDING, HE WAS ALREADY DEAD. SOURCES TELL THE BOSTON GLOBE THAT RAYNE AND COLE WERE SCHEDULED TO BE MARRIED NEXT MONTH.

Underneath the short article was the same picture Rose had

described to me. It showed Alix in the middle of the road, holding Dylan against her chest.

That photo had become the face of the bombing.

It was no wonder she had so many followers online.

And why she only posted sunny days.

I clicked the screen off and put my phone away.

I couldn't look at it anymore.

The pain on her face fucking killed me.

I got up and started pacing the room, trying to remember the first time I had seen that photo published. I had been in Dubai during the bombing on a two-week vacation, and I'd followed the story from the other side of the world. And, when I'd returned to Boston, I had been focused on how they were going to prosecute the motherfucker who hadn't died during the shoot-out.

Even though I'd seen the picture before, I'd had no idea Alix was in the photo.

I turned at the wall and started walking back toward Rose, my hands tugging at my hair, trying to process everything I'd seen today.

Rose's hands were pressed against her chest, holding the blanket the nurse had given to us because we were both soaked.

I cleared my throat and stopped a few feet in front of her. "Was April 15 the last day Alix was a paramedic?" I asked.

Rose nodded, giving me the answer I'd feared. "She was one of the best in the city. She tried so hard to get back to it. Every couple of weeks, she'd go to the firehouse, but she just couldn't do it."

She glanced up, our eyes finally connecting. I knew my expression looked as emotional as hers.

"She took a year off and just recently went back to work. She wanted to stay in emergency services, so she transferred to the call center."

"That's not easy either." I scraped my fingers through my

beard as I pictured her answering the phone. "She probably worries every day that she'll get a call, and it will send her into a flashback, like thunder does."

"I've never thought about that," Rose admitted. "But, my God, you're probably right."

Jesus Christ.

We both turned quiet again.

There was nothing left to say.

And I started to pace once more.

I just wanted to help her.

Heal her.

Make her pain go away.

But I couldn't do a goddamn thing in this room besides walk back and forth across the fucking floor and wait for a doctor to come out and tell me if Alix was all right.

FIFTY-FOUR

DYLAN

I WALKED over to Alix's hospital bed and sat on the very edge, surrounding her hand with mine. There was an IV in her wrist and oxygen in her nose.

Physically, she was going to be fine.

She would stay the night here, and in the morning, she would be good to go home.

But, mentally, she was putting up one hell of a fight.

It was my fault.

I was selfish.

I didn't want to let her go.

Alix Rayne was the love of my life.

She was my balance.

The air I flew through.

The sun that shone during every sunny day.

It hurt to be without her.

To watch her live a life that she should have been sharing with me.

But she wasn't really living because I wouldn't let her.

I knew how hard she was struggling.

I knew the position I was putting her in.

I didn't care.

Even when she'd broken down, when she'd walked three and a half miles across the city to find me, a place she hadn't visited since the funeral, she couldn't say good-bye.

She was too loyal.

She would continue to grasp at any bit of hope I threw at her.

And she wouldn't stop.

Because she was a fighter.

A survivor.

A healer.

Someone who didn't let go.

I had to be the one.

And I had to do it now.

I leaned my face close to hers and breathed her in.

Lemon.

The scent of the ambulance had stuck to her skin the whole time we'd been together, just like it was on her now.

I would miss that smell.

I'd miss her.

"Alix," I whispered.

Slowly, there was movement. It started in her feet and legs and went to her arms and hands. Her eyes gradually opened, and she took in my face.

She smiled.

I knew she didn't realize she was in a hospital. I was sure she wouldn't remember leaving the townhouse and walking to the cemetery or falling asleep at my grave.

I wasn't going to mention it.

There were plenty of people in the waiting room who could fill her in.

My time with her was limited, and I didn't want to waste a second.

"Hi," she said so softly, the color finally returning to her skin. "You're so beautiful."

It was true.

And she had to know.

Because this was the last time I would ever be able to tell her.

Her cheeks blushed, her smile not fading at all.

I would miss that, too.

"My Alix," I started. My fingers stretched out over her hand, gently touching the wire of the IV. "I told you once that you were in my life for only two seconds when I knew I loved you."

"That's what I used to measure almost everything by, comparing it all to two seconds." Her voice was hoarse, but I knew it would come back to normal soon. "If someone can love that deep in that short amount of time, then two seconds isn't really quick at all."

She was right.

It had only taken one second for my entire life to pass before my eyes.

And another to hit the ground.

"You're going to have so many more seconds in your life."

"We are," she corrected me.

I smiled at her. "We had some good ones, didn't we?"

She nodded, a tear dropping each time she lifted her head. "They were incredible."

"I remember the lunch we had in the park the day of the marathon," I told her. "You were sitting in front of me, and your back was leaning into my chest. I put my lips on top of your head, and I was thinking of how lucky I was to be there with you. How, in just a month's time, you were going to be my wife. And, while I was sitting there, I pictured our future. What it would be like to see you pregnant and giving birth to our child. What it would be like to see that baby graduate from college. How many times a month you could get my ass up Cadillac Mountain once we retired."

She laughed, and it was beautiful.

"I never pictured a moment that didn't have you in it. My life started when I met you. And I consider myself the luckiest man in the world because my life ended with you."

I couldn't catch her tears, as they were moving far too fast, so I just let them fall.

"Dylan," she wept.

She knew.

I could see it in her eyes.

"Alix, I have to let you go."

She was shaking her head, but she was saying, "I know."

She was torn down the middle.

Once again.

She would never make this decision.

So, I would.

"I want you to smile again. I want you to get back in that ambulance and do what you love because you don't know when that choice is going to be taken away from you. I want you to live."

"You can't go."

"If I keep holding on, you're going to lose everything you have. I won't let that happen. You've already lost enough."

She looked down at my hand, her thumb grazing over the back of my palm. "What if I forget?"

"You won't."

"How do you know that, Dylan? Because, right now, I can close my eyes and I can see the texture of your skin and I can hear the exact pitch of your voice and I can perfectly describe the scent of your cologne. It's all so fresh in my mind. But what if those memories dull? What if I need your laughter to get me through the saddest day, and I can't hear it anymore? What if I need you to hold my hand, and I can't remember what your fingers looked like?"

I reached up and touched the side of her head. "All of that is right in here. You might have to dig, but you'll always find it."

I brought her hand up to my lips, and I kissed her fingertips. She had the softest skin.

That was something else I'd miss.

"It's time."

"Wait," she cried out. "How am I supposed to say good-bye when I know I'll never see you again?"

She knew she would see me in pictures and in memories.

She had those now.

She also knew she would be with me again.

So, there was only one way to answer her.

I pressed my lips against hers and whispered, "I love you, Alix."

She closed her eyes, her tears soaking my mouth, her lips quivering between mine, and said, "I love you, too."

She didn't open her lids for two seconds.

By then, I was already gone.

FIFTY-FIVE

ALIX

PRESENT DAY

I FELT A TINGLING.

It started in my feet and moved to my legs. It then traveled to my arms and hands. Warmth was spreading throughout me as I regained the feeling in my body.

The darkness behind my lids was lightening as I lifted them. Slowly.

The light immediately stung.

It felt as though it had been months since I saw it.

Maybe a year—a time frame that felt almost exact.

As my vision became more focused, I saw a face staring back at me.

At first, I thought it was Dylan.

I expected it to be him since I'd just seen him two seconds ago.

He had told me he loved me and ...

It suddenly all came back to me.

The conversation we'd had.

The good-bye.

But Dylan wasn't whom I was looking at right now.

It was Smith.

I squeezed his fingers as they clung to my left hand, hoping to alleviate the worry in his expression. "I'm okay."

My throat burned.

My voice was raspy.

"That's what the doctor said, too." He moved closer. I could almost feel the heat from his body even though only his hand was touching me. "They're going to keep you overnight. As long as your vitals stay normal, you'll be discharged in the morning."

It took me a minute to register what he'd said.

"The doctor?" I asked.

I looked past him and saw the room, the gown I was dressed in, the machines on the side of me, the IV in my hand.

I was in the hospital.

But why?

I felt my blood pressure spike as the panic began to set in.

Rose was walking over to the bed, wearing the same expression Smith had on. She took my right hand and said, "Do you remember?"

As I glanced at her face, I tried to rewind to the last memory I had.

I'd taken a shower and gotten dressed to go to Smith's house.

Rose had sent me a text, saying it was going to rain.

I'd walked out my front door and stood on the steps.

I couldn't recall a single detail after that.

"No," I admitted, "I don't remember."

"We don't have to talk about it now," Smith said. "We just got you back. We need to make sure you're feeling all right, and then, when you're up to it, we can discuss everything that happened tonight."

I'd scared them.

I could tell that by the way they were looking at me.

The truth was, there were days when I scared myself.

Every storm that came through.

Every *craaack* that filled my ears.

"Where was I when you found me?" I asked.

Because someone had to have found me.

That was how I'd gotten to the hospital.

"Alix, you don't need to worry about this right now," Smith said.

"Yes, I do!" I shouted. "I have to know."

"We found you in front of Dylan's grave," Rose said.

As each word entered my chest, it tightened around my heart.

"You were unconscious."

And then it felt like my heart stopped beating.

The sound of her voice told me the scene had been ugly.

The terror in her eyes told me I'd done more than just frighten her.

"Did you go to my townhouse first?" I asked.

I knew the answer.

I just needed to hear it.

When Smith nodded, I wanted to throw up.

I wanted to crawl off this bed and go into the bathroom and never come out.

I wanted to scream, so I slapped my hand over my mouth to keep it in.

My fingers didn't stop the tears.

They dripped over the back of my palm.

They made everything blurry.

I finally looked at Rose and pulled my fingers away and admitted, "I've been hiding this from you."

Each syllable stabbed my chest.

They caused my breathing to become more labored.

She put both hands around mine. "I realized that once I was inside your house."

"I'm sorry, Rose. I'm so sorry I didn't tell you."

"I know, babe."

Gradually, my gaze shifted to Smith. It hurt just as much to say to him, "I couldn't let you see the truth." And, before either of them could interject, I added, "I know I need help. I can't do this anymore. It's controlling my life, and it's far bigger than me."

I'd known that for a while.

I just wasn't ready.

Looking at their faces, waking up in the hospital, had changed that.

Smith had changed that, too.

I knew I couldn't give him all of me unless I let Dylan go.

"Oh, thank God," Rose groaned with relief. "You have no idea how badly I wanted to hear you say that."

Never once had she ever kept her feelings from me.

I didn't want her to start now.

"I should have gotten help when I first lost him," I told them.

"It's okay," Rose said. "I can understand why it took you so long to want it."

My voice was so soft when I confessed, "I wasn't prepared to face it, but I am now."

"I'm so proud of you, it hurts, and I love you so ridiculously much." She stood and leaned down to kiss my forehead. Then, she turned to Smith and said, "I'm going to go get us some coffee and see if I can snag us some scrubs, so we can get out of these wet clothes."

Smith thanked her before his attention returned to me.

That was when I noticed he was soaked—his jeans, jacket, even the ends of his hair.

I had a feeling that was because of me.

He'd been out in the rain.

He'd seen my storm.

I was embarrassed he'd witnessed those secrets.

And I was relieved that I didn't have to carry those secrets anymore.

But, now, I was worried he would leave me.

That I was far too damaged for him to love.

That thought seared across my heart.

"I'm sorry I scared you," I said as the tears continued to fall.

He reached toward my face, his fingers softly wiping the wetness off my cheeks.

"You're safe. You're going to be okay. That's all that matters."

I took a breath and the air got stuck in my throat. My nose was running. My lips were trembling so hard I was sure they'd never be still again. "I-I couldn't tell you, Smith. I couldn't t-tell anyone."

"You don't have to justify—"

"You d-deserve an explanation, and I'm going t-to give you one." I twisted my engagement ring that wasn't there, and I attempted to calm my breathing. And as I stared as Smith's handsome face, I tried to find a way to explain something that was indescribable. "When I found Dylan, I couldn't help him. He was dead in my arms and I lost it and ..." I stopped to swallow, the spit becoming so thick in my mouth from how hard I was still crying. "Keeping Dylan close, keeping his things in my house, it made me feel just the tiniest bit normal, like the bomb had never gone off, like everything was the same as it had always been." The air burned my lungs as I sucked it in. "I wasn't living. I know that now. In fact, I was barely surviving. And then I met you, and I was ripping myself in half; part of me was still in the past, and the other was with you in the present."

His hand cupped my cheek. "I knew, when I eventually saw your storm, I would get all of you. Even if that took forever, I would have waited."

"You're so good to me."

The last time I had said that was when he'd wanted to take me to Lake Tahoe.

I'd meant it.

I meant it even more now.

I glanced at the end of the bed where my toes were sticking into the blanket. They were so sore, and I didn't know why. But they reminded me of a question Smith had once asked me. A question I had to ask him now because I honestly didn't know the answer. "Don't you want to run?"

He brought my fingers up to his mouth and kissed them.

Dylan had done the same thing just a few moments ago.

I knew that thought should be clenching my heart.

But it wasn't.

"No, I don't want to run," he said. "Unless it's toward you, and then my answer is yes."

FIFTY-SIX
SMITH
PRESENT DAY

I STOOD in the living room of Alix's townhouse, glancing around at the emptiness. There wasn't any furniture in here, and nothing was on the walls. Once the property had gone into escrow, Alix had donated all of the furnishings to several different sober living houses throughout Boston. One of the places was where Joe was living now that he'd completed rehab.

The closing was scheduled for tomorrow, and Alix wanted to just stop in one last time.

She wanted a good-bye.

Rose and I had met her here.

Rose had brought champagne and three glasses, and it was waiting for us in the kitchen.

I'd recently learned all about moments.

This was one.

And we were going to celebrate it.

As Alix walked down the stairs, there was a smile on her face.

It was different than the grins I'd seen in the past.

It was raw.

It was the look someone gave when they reached the other side and could smile over what they had overcome.

Not everyone fought.

Not everyone knew how good that could feel.

Alix did.

She had begun the battle over one of the biggest wars.

And she was fucking brawling.

Like Boston.

Because that girl was Boston Strong.

She had a therapist and was now four months deep into treating her PTSD.

With the help of her doctor, one of the first big decisions she'd made was to sell the townhouse she'd shared with Dylan. Her name was on the deed, so it was hers to do whatever she wanted with it. She had gotten a full-price offer within two days.

She'd quickly found a place to rent that was just a few streets over from here. It was a one-bedroom apartment, a fourth of the size of her townhouse.

It was perfect for her.

One day, she'd live with me, but it wasn't the right time for that.

She was still getting stronger.

She was still learning who she really was.

And I couldn't be more in love with the person she was becoming.

"Hi," she said as she joined me in the living room, linking her hand with mine.

"Are you all right?"

She nodded. "It hurts to be back here, but I'm okay." She glanced up at the ceiling and briefly around the room. "I'm glad to be moving on."

"I don't know about you bitches, but I need a cocktail," Rose whined in the background.

Alix and I laughed, and we followed Rose into the kitchen where she poured champagne into the three glasses and gave us each one.

"To moments," Rose said, holding hers up in the air.

"To moments," Alix repeated.

I watched as she clinked her glass against Rose's.

I listened to the carefree sound that came out of her mouth.

I tasted the flavor of the champagne on her lips when I reached forward and kissed her.

She put her hand on my face, and a full smile spread across her lips.

She didn't say it.

She didn't have to.

I saw it in her eyes.

And mine said it right back to her.

EPILOGUE

ALIX — ONE YEAR LATER

I'D THOUGHT good-bye was forever.

I'd thought, once those words were spoken, there was no going back.

But Dylan had taught me that wasn't true.

Because, even though he'd said that to me in the hospital, he was still very much a part of my life.

The difference was, now, he was just a memory.

And I had so many of them.

After his death, I had said good-bye to Bar Harbor. I no longer felt a connection to it. I couldn't fathom stepping inside our house.

So, I put it on the market.

Fortunately, it never sold, and I'd decided to keep it.

It had taken a long time before I could make the drive to Maine. Before I could hold the keys in my hand. Before I could walk through the door.

Before I felt like it was a place I could love again.

But I had gotten there.

And, even though it was a home I'd shared with Dylan, it was never what he wanted.

Therefore, it felt like mine.

After several trips up north, I'd finally had the courage to climb Cadillac Mountain.

It took some physical training. My body hadn't attempted anything that rigorous in a while.

But I had already been in that mode because I had qualified to run the Boston Marathon.

And I'd crossed the finish line.

Some of the loudest people cheering for me at the end had been the guys from engine thirty-three, ladder fifteen. The firehouse on Boylston Street. The one I'd worked at before the bombing.

And the one I worked at now.

I'd taken a few days off from the station to come up to Maine, and this was my third morning here. I'd gotten up at a little past three to start the climb up the mountain.

Instead of sitting on the rock where Dylan had proposed, I went to the other side of the summit. I stood close to the edge, and I looked down at the elevation. Then, I glanced at the water, and I breathed in the Maine air.

I'd missed it here.

And I missed Dylan.

I always would.

But the misery didn't own me like it once had.

They were just thoughts I had of him. I would acknowledge them, and then I could move on.

Still, every time I was up here, looking at the sunrise like I was now, I swore, I saw his face in the sun.

It made me smile.

But that wasn't the only reason I was grinning.

Smith's hands were wrapping around my waist, and he was pressing his lips against the side of my neck.

He was still so gentle and so sexy at the same time.

"It's going to be a sunny day," he whispered in my ear.

I was so thankful for that.

Maybe, one day, I would love the rain, but I was still learning how to handle the storm.

AUTHOR'S NOTE

The idea for this book came to me in February 2017. I had just lost my grandmother, who I called my best friend, who meant everything to me. I didn't know how to cope. I didn't know how to grieve. I didn't know how to exist in a world that no longer had her in it.

The only thing I knew was how badly I missed her and how I just wanted one more moment with her.

A few nights after she passed away, I started writing, but not a book. The words I put down were for me. My fingers tapping the keys was the only thing that made me feel normal. That night, I emptied my soul. I purged every emotion I was feeling. And I answered the questions that had been haunting me. If I were given just a few more moments, what would they look like? How would I feel? Would I get the closure I needed?

When Ashes Fall was born.

It took seventeen months before I could emotionally tackle this novel, but every single word I wrote that night is in the book you just read.

This story gave me the moment I needed. It gave me extra

time with my grandmother. It allowed me to grieve. It taught me how to cope. And it helped me heal.

My grandmother was from Boston—a city I began visiting when I was just a few months old—and when I graduated college, I was able to call it home. I lived in the Back Bay. I visited every place that is mentioned in this book.

Although I don't live there now, Boston is such a big part of my history. And, because it was my grandmother's birthplace, it felt like the right backdrop for this story.

One thing I've learned throughout this entire journey is, tragedy affects everyone differently. No two experiences are alike. Pain is pain, and it can be debilitating.

Please don't ever be afraid to ask for help.

You don't have to do this alone.

Boston Strong.

XO,

Marni

Veterans Crisis Line: (800) 273-TALK
PTSD Foundation of America: (877) 717-PTSD
National Suicide Prevention Lifeline: (800) 273-8255

ACKNOWLEDGMENTS

Jovana Shirley, I can't thank you enough for changing your entire schedule to fit me in. You're always there for me, always willing to do whatever you can to make things work. I say this every time and at the end of each book, the statement couldn't be truer—I would never want to do this with anyone but you. Love you.

Nina Grinstead, I love you more than anything. You're the most amazing publicist and friend, and I can't thank you enough for being on this journey with me.

Judy Zweifel, as always, thank you for being so wonderful to work with and for taking such good care of my words. <3

Kaitie Reister, I love you, girl, so hard. You're my biggest cheerleader, and you're such a wonderful friend. Thank you for being you. XO

Letitia, thank you for creating a face for this book that's better than I could have ever dreamed of.

Crystal Radaker, my dark-souled sister, this one almost killed us. But we got to the end, and you're the reason I made it. You believed in this book and you believed in me and you fought to make it the best. I'm forever grateful for everything you do for my books and for being the most incredible friend to me. I love you so much.

Kimmi Street, I love that we're on this journey together. You're the sister I never had and the best friend I always wanted. I love us. And I love you.

Nikki Terrill and Andrea Lefkowitz, I don't know what I would do without you two. Your support, love, encouragement, virtual wine—it's all so appreciated. You girls never left my side the whole time I was writing this book, and I will never forget that. I love you both.

Ratula Roy, I love you to death. Every email, every voice memo, every PM you send makes my whole world. Thank you for being a part of this.

Ricky, my sexyreads, we're in this until the end, baby. Love you.

Rachel Van Dyken, I'm so grate for all of your help and advice and words of encouragement. Thank you will never be enough.

Melissa Mann, thank you for the gorgeous quote. It inspired so much of this story. I'm so grateful you let me use it.

Gia Riley, thank you for always keeping me laughing. It means more than you'll ever know. Chomp.

Extra-special love goes to Chanpreet Singh, Hilary Suppes, Donna Cooksley Sanderson, Stacey Jacovina, Jesse James, Kayti McGee, Carol Nevarez, Julie Vaden, Elizabeth Kelley, Jennifer Porpora, Melissa Mann, Pat Mann, Katie Amanatidis, Katy Truscott, my COPA ladies, and my group of Sarasota girls whom I love more than anything. I'm so grateful for all of you.

Mom and Dad, thanks for your unwavering belief in me and your constant encouragement. It means more than you'll ever know.

Brian, my words could never dent the amount of love you give me. Trust me when I say, I love you more.

My Midnighters, you are such a supportive, loving, motivating group. Thanks for being such an inspiration, for holding my hand when I need it, and for always begging for more words. I love you all.

To all the bloggers who read, review, share, post, tweet, Instagram—Thank you, thank you, thank you. You do so much for our writing community, and we're so appreciative.

To my readers—I cherish each and every one of you. I'm so grateful for all the love you show my books, for taking the time to reach out to me, and for your passion and enthusiasm. I love, love, love you.

Lastly, I want to thank the city of Boston. You've served as an inspiration for so many of my books. Your energy, your spirit, your charisma are unlike any other place in the world. Boston Strong. Always.

MARNI'S MIDNIGHTERS

Getting to know my readers is one of my favorite parts about being an author. In Marni's Midnighters, my private Facebook group, we chat about steamy books, sexy and taboo toys, and sensual book boyfriends. Team members also qualify for exclusive giveaways and are the first to receive sneak peeks of the projects I'm currently working on. To join Marni's Midnighters, click HERE.

ABOUT THE AUTHOR

Best-selling author Marni Mann knew she was going to be a writer since middle school. While other girls her age were daydreaming about teenage pop stars, Marni was fantasizing about penning her first novel. She crafts sexy, titillating stories that weave together her love of darkness, mystery, passion, and human emotions. A New Englander at heart, she now lives in Sarasota, Florida, with her husband and their two dogs. When she's not nose deep in her laptop, working on her next novel, she's scouring for chocolate, sipping wine, traveling, or devouring fabulous books.

Want to get in touch? Visit Marni at ...
www.marnismann.com
MarniMannBooks@gmail.com

ALSO BY MARNI MANN

STAND-ALONE NOVELS

The Assistant (Contemporary Romance)

The Unblocked Collection (Erotic Romance)

Wild Aces (Erotic Romance)

Prisoned (Dark Erotic Thriller)

THE AGENCY STAND-ALONE SERIES—Erotic Romance

Signed

Endorsed

Contracted

Negotiated

THE SHADOWS SERIES—Erotic Romance

Seductive Shadows—Book One

Seductive Secrecy—Book Two

THE PRISONED SPIN-OFF DUET—Dark Erotic Thriller

Animal—Book One

Monster—Book Two

THE BAR HARBOR SERIES—New Adult

Pulled Beneath—Book One

Pulled Within—Book Two

THE MEMOIR SERIES—Dark Mainstream Fiction

Memoirs Aren't Fairytales—Book One

Scars from a Memoir—Book Two

NOVELS COWRITTEN WITH GIA RILEY

Lover (Erotic Romance)

Drowning (Contemporary Romance)

SNEAK PEEK OF MEMOIRS AREN'T FAIRYTALES

CHAPTER ONE

ERIC SAT behind the wheel of his beat-up '89 Toyota Corolla. His seat was so close to the steering wheel that his knees hit the dashboard, and he couldn't see out the rearview mirror. He hadn't complained once about having no legroom or that his back was slumped forward because there was an enormous box of clothes behind his seat. His lips were stuck in a perma-grin, and his eyes were wide and glued to the taillights of the car ahead.

It had taken us almost six hours to reach the border between New Hampshire and Massachusetts when it should have taken less than four. Eric said the Rabbit—what he had named his Corolla because the thing wouldn't die, like in those battery commercials—topped out at sixty. I didn't think all the extra weight was healthy for the Rabbit either. I could hear the poor thing chugging.

Eric had emptied his entire bedroom and packed it all into the backseat and trunk. A lampshade teetering on top of a pile of clothes kept jabbing into my head, and the corner of his TV rubbed against my elbow. But I didn't complain either.

I hadn't put that much thought into packing. I grabbed some

pants from my closet and some dirty shirts that were on my floor. I swiped a few toiletries from the bathroom and crammed it all into two backpacks. The ounce of weed I'd scored the night before went into my purse, and that was all I brought.

No one ever left Bangor; we called it The Hole. There was something about the place that sucked you in and kept you in shackles. If you went away for college, you never came back. If you stayed in state, like Eric and me, you were a Bangor lifer. No matter how much money you tried to save or plans you put together, you'd end up, years later, married to someone you met in high school, with kids, a Labrador, and a Cape Cod house. And then it was too late to leave. You had to escape as a teenager. It was the only way.

Two weeks earlier, Eric and I had been sitting in his car. It was late at night, and we were passing a bowl between us. He went on about his dead-end job at the auto repair shop, never having any money, and the nerve of his parents for charging him rent. My advice had always been the same. I told him to go back to college. He never should have dropped out in the first place.

But that night, my advice was different.

A month before, I'd dropped out of the University of Maine, halfway through the spring semester of my sophomore year. I'd quit my job at the campus coffee shop, too. And since then, I hadn't done much besides sit on my parents' couch and watch TV all day. I was ready for a change.

After the third bowl and a couple shots of some peppermint shit, I said, "If you hate it here so much, then move. I'll go with you."

He sat silent for a minute, then he pulled out his wallet and slapped forty bucks on the armrest.

We were almost out of weed, and it was his turn to buy.

"Let's go," he said.

He was the one driving, so I looked at him to start the car.

"I mean it, let's get the fuck out of here," he said.

And then he started talking so fast it was like he was rapping along to the Jay-Z song on the radio. I couldn't even get a word in. He was going to pick a city along the East Coast and find us a cheap apartment to rent. He would give notice at his job and save the next paycheck, and in two weeks, we'd be out.

He showed up at my house the next morning with coffee and bagels, and we ate breakfast on my bed. He was quiet and ate his bagel really slow.

I knew Eric too well. We'd been best friends since kindergarten and even dated for a week in the fourth grade.

So, when he started fumbling with my comforter and acting all antsy, I knew he was getting ready to tell me we couldn't leave until he saved more money.

I was dead wrong.

Under his jacket, he had hidden a bunch of papers. He'd stayed up all night, researching different places to live and apartments to rent. He'd wanted to surprise me. And he did.

We were moving to Boston into a studio apartment in Chinatown, and all he needed from me was half the security deposit and a yes. I gave him both.

I didn't know what our apartment looked like. I'd never been to Chinatown before, and I didn't care. We were approaching the Tobin Bridge, and for the first time since I'd moved back in with my parents, I felt free.

At the start of the bridge, my hands grabbed the support bar on the door. Eric's hands were on ten and two, his knuckles white. It was like we were strapped in a cart, riding up to the peak of a roller coaster. The skyline of Boston was in front of us, and somewhere in the middle of all those tall buildings was the place we were going to call home.

Eric shouted over the music, "We did it, Nicole! We're here!"

All four windows were open, and I leaned my head against

the back of the seat. My eyes closed. Wind was rushing through the car, filling it with the smell of smog and fish from the Mystic River.

A clothes hanger was tickling the side of my ear and pulling out strands of my ponytail every time we went over a bump. The metal was cold, and as it touched my hair, it reminded me of my mom's cool hands, brushing the hair out of my face and tucking it behind my ear when she put me to bed as a child.

My hands let go of the bar, and I put my arms up in the air, feeling the breeze swish between my fingers. "Hell yeah, we did," I said.

If you would like to keep reading, click HERE *to purchase Memoirs Aren't Fairytales.*